# The Cases of Owen Barham

by
Darin Fortner

This is a work of fiction. Names, characters, places, and incidents are either the product of the author's imagination or are used fictitiously, and any resemblance to actual persons living or dead, business establishments, events, or locales, is entirely coincidental.

**The Cases of Owen Barham**

COPYRIGHT © 2026 by Darin Fortner

All rights reserved. No part of this book may be used or reproduced in any manner whatsoever without written permission of the author except in the case of brief quotations embodied in critical articles or reviews.

Art Effects by Sarah Fortner
Cover Photo by Boston Public Library, Md Shariful Islam, Aaron Burden on Unsplash
Title Page Photos by Jack Finnigan, Jose Castillo, Matt Jones, Andrew Neel, Tomasz Zielonka, The Australian National Maritime Museum, Jose Duarte, Randy Jacob, "Michael", Cassiano K Wehr, Chris Haws, Daniel Lincoln, Fleur Stolk, Gerald Bost on Unsplash

Publishing History
First Edition, 2026
Paperback ISBN 9798251736946

Published in the United States of America

# A WORD FROM THE AUTHOR

Have you, dear reader, ever wondered what it would be like to experience life in the past? Imagine, for instance, that you set out on a journey by train into London—only to discover, when you at last stepped onto the platform at Paddington Station, that time had rolled back 100 years. What would your surroundings look like, sound like, smell like? What would the newspaper articles detail? And, as a mystery enthusiast, if you approached the bookseller's stall, what tales would be available for you to read?

This volume is, in a sense, an answer to that last question. The following thirteen stories are written in the style and language of the period, as if drawn from the pages of some forgotten magazine. They describe the adventures of university student Owen Barham as he unravels peculiar riddles, impossible disappearances, and bizarre crimes of all stripes—in short, the sort of mysteries popular in the 1920s.

We hope you enjoy this little trip into another time. Share your thoughts and comments with us at:

www.facebook.com/FortnerCreations

# The Cases of Owen Barham

The Undersecretary's Umbrella ...................... 3

The Vanishing of Valdonato ......................... 27

The Wainwright Will ..................................... 53

The Xanthic Xenophon ................................. 69

The Yews of Yarborough............................... 89

The Zealot of Zachary ................................ 109

The False Mr. Fordham............................... 127

The Absence of the Assassin ...................... 147

The Broken Blade ....................................... 163

The Clue of the Camera ............................. 181

The Deity of Durian .................................... 195

The Error in the Evidence .......................... 211

The Galthorpe Gemini ................................ 223

"So in conclusion, gentlemen, you have made no progress."

On a gusty spring morning in 192-, in a corner room on the top floor of Swansea's central police station, in the office of the Chief Constable, four men were gathered. The Chief Constable himself, a heavy man with short-cropped grey hair, had his hands folded together on his desk and a frown on his wide face. Seated before him were Inspector Sedlock of the Special Branch, sharp-featured and keen-eyed, and Chief Inspector Jones of the Swansea Borough Police, whose plump frame was capped with curly black locks. The fourth man, and the speaker, was a Mr. Snow of the Home Office, who was standing at the window with his back to the others and his hands clasped behind him. The sky was full of small clouds scudding along, and now and again a break in their ranks permitted a touch of sunshine to gleam through and set the ancient chimneypots aglow; but his mind was not on the beauty of the scene.

Exactly one week earlier a crime had occurred that was dramatic enough, and had such potentially wide-reaching ramifications for His Majesty's Government, that there had been an immediate spasm in Downing Street, and Mr. Snow and Inspector Sedlock had been sent straightaway to Swansea to oversee the investigation. Despite knowing the identity of the culprit and the circumstances of the crime, however, a solution remained maddeningly out of reach.

Chief Inspector Jones cleared his throat. His role thus far had been limited in the main to making himself and his men available to carry out Inspector Sedlock's directions, but he was not a petty man, and he was as keen as any of them to bring the case to a successful conclusion.

"I have a suggestion," he said. "This is an unusual crime, and it may be time for us to look for help from an unusual source. There's a group of students in the city for a tour of architectural sites, from University College London, and one of them is the young man who helped solve the Lendrich case about a year ago…"

Sedlock lifted his head, with the manner of a pointer catching sight of quarry. "The Niles Lendrich case? The murdered architect?"

"You've heard of it, then, Inspector?" Snow asked, turning from the window. "I have not, and despite whatever ratiocinative interest the episode may undoubtedly have had, can you seriously be considering applying for assistance from a mere student? I must most strenuously question the propriety of involving an outsider in a matter as sensitive as this…"

"As you said," returned the Chief Constable, "we've made no progress so far. What harm can it do us at this point to have another opinion? All right, Jones, you bring this boy here, and we'll see what he has to say."

"I know just where their group is now, sir," Jones said, pushing himself up from his chair. "I'll have him here within the hour."

True to his word, Jones ushered into the room about forty minutes later a slender young man who could hardly have been a day over twenty, with pale blond hair brushed straight back from his forehead and light blue eyes that looked out from behind round spectacles. His voice was soft but precise, and despite his educated diction Sedlock thought he detected a hint of Bow Bells in his speech.

"This is Owen Barham," the chief inspector said simply.

After brief introductions had been made all around, and the lad was settled in the chair Jones dragged forward for him, Mr. Snow took up the mantle of explanation, with his usual brusqueness.

"I trust Chief Inspector Jones has given you some idea of the reason you were sent for? Due to considerations of state I cannot go into complete details of the problem facing us, but I have been informed that you have experience untangling similar conundrums, and perhaps with the limited information I am able to impart to you, you will at least be inspired to suggest a method of approach to a solution.

"For the past six months the Admiralty has had a naval engineering venture underway here in Swansea, headquartered at Penryn House. This undertaking had reached its halfway point, and after weeks of research and calculation the resulting designs were committed to paper, when the blueprints of a key component were stolen.

"Allow me to describe to you the security measures taken for this enterprise. The five men working on it were assigned the third floor of Penryn House, for their use and theirs alone. There is no lift at Penryn House; the only apparent way to access the third floor is by means of the staircase at the front of the building. All windows on the third floor have been painted shut. Immediately on the right, past the third-floor landing, is a small alcove with a table, and upon that table a register. All persons visiting the third floor are obliged to sign in upon arrival and sign out upon their departure. In addition–and this restriction extends all the way to the head of the committee–anyone leaving the third floor, even for a short time, is required to submit to a search of his person by one of the two guards on duty, to the extent of emptying his pockets completely and being tested down to his underclothing. No papers of any sort, nor anything capable of carrying papers, is allowed to be taken from the third floor until this project is concluded.

"Nevertheless, a week ago, a crucial technical drawing was removed. Of the five members of the third-floor staff, four have been accounted for at the time of the theft. The head of the committee, Sir Henry Cathcart, an Undersecretary of the Admiralty, locked the collected designs in the safe in his office before heading downstairs to the dining hall a few minutes after noon. He never left the building during the time of the theft. Mr. Rhys Griffiths and Colonel Haydn Vaughan had already made their way down to the first floor, at approximately eleven-fifty, and they likewise did not leave the building during the time of the crime. The next member of Sir Henry's staff, Mr. Bradley Teal, went down to the dining hall about five or ten minutes after his employer, and like the rest he was thoroughly searched before leaving the third floor, and could not have carried the missing paper away.

"That leaves the final member of the committee, young Mr. David Coughanowr. His office is on the same side of the corridor as Sir Henry's, with a connecting door between them, meaning that he could easily have stepped through and burgled Sir Henry's safe at any time during the interval. Too, it was raining heavily on the day of the theft, and Sir Henry noticed upon returning to his office that his umbrella, which he had loaned to Coughanowr for the young man's use that day, was coated with water, proving that he had exited the building at some point.

"We do not know how Coughanowr gained access to Sir Henry's safe, we do not know how he left Penryn House with the stolen plans, but he is the only possible suspect. For the past week Chief Inspector Jones's men have followed Coughanowr on his daily rounds, but he has not contacted any suspicious characters or behaved in an unusual manner. What we want from you is to tell us how the missing design was absconded, if you can, but far more importantly, how we can retrieve it before it passes into the hands of a foreign agent. Have you any questions?"

Their young visitor had listened to the account with his head lowered and his eyes on the tips of his shoes, and he inquired, without looking up, "Am I permitted to ask what the missing paper depicts?"

"I hardly think that information is germane to recovering it," Snow replied coolly. "Apart from stating that the completed plans are of a new component that will be crucial in naval warfare in the coming years, I will say this: any number of foreign powers would pay dearly to purchase the missing design, and it is imperative that we recover it immediately."

"And why work on this project here in Swansea?"

"Aside from the committee's having access to the resources of the University College and the Royal Institute of South Wales, Swansea has several foundries and an excellent harbour. Not to mention that a village in Wales is hardly the first place foreign agents would normally think to look for the latest development in Brittania's defenses."

Barham, lifting his head, asked, "You're certain the missing plan's been taken from Penryn House? It couldn't have been simply destroyed, or hidden somewhere in the building?"

"As soon as Sir Henry discovered the paper was missing," Inspector Sedlock broke in, "he had his staff search the entire third floor, room by room, before notifying his superiors of the theft. When I and my men arrived in Swansea, we examined the third floor ourselves, and then proceeded on to search every inch of the rest of Penryn House. We found nothing. Penryn House was recently converted to central heating, and its flues were bricked up. Anyone who tried to burn papers in its fireplaces would get a nasty surprise, and we found no evidence to suggest that anything vital had been burned recently on the third floor, or cut into pieces, or torn apart. There are no secret passages or sliding panels or ingenious hiding places. The windows on the third floor, as Mr. Snow pointed out, have been sealed shut, and can't be opened enough to even slide a piece of notepaper out. Apparently, in some way none of the rest of us can fathom, young Coughanowr simply walked out of the building with the paper tucked under his arm somehow, and no one noticed."

"Could one or both of the guards on duty on the third floor that day been bribed to say they saw nothing?"

"As distasteful as such a suggestion is," said Mr. Snow– "the guards at Penryn House being handpicked as representing the finest from among His Majesty's Royal Marines–the possibility has not been overlooked. Inspector Sedlock has thoroughly examined the finances of the two men who were on duty on the day of the theft, and not a farthing has been found out of place. No, the answer to this problem lies elsewhere."

"How large is the missing paper?"

Snow made a quick, sharp gesture with both hands, describing a space roughly the size of a folio. "The plans aren't something that can be easily carried about in one's pockets, if that's what you have in mind."

"How are they normally transported?" asked Barham.

"The usual method, as far as I understand it, is to roll them and carry them in a pasteboard cylinder."

"They're never folded?"

"I should think it highly unlikely."

"Were there any visitors to the third floor of Penryn House on the day of the theft, anyone who wouldn't normally have been there?"

"Visitors to the committee are few, and their visits brief. There was only one on the day in question, Lord R–" –here Snow mentioned a distinguished and highly eminent member of Parliament, a man almost as far above reproach as the King himself– "and that was in the morning, hours before the theft. The full complement of plans was still in Sir Henry's possession when His Lordship made his departure."

"What does Mr. Coughanowr claim he was doing while the theft occurred?"

"Supposedly he was at his desk in the next room the entire time, copying certain nonessential papers for a trial exercise to be held the following day. He had, in fact, sent down to the dining hall for some sandwiches, and a boy was sent up to the third floor with a tray at roughly twelve-fifteen. The boy never saw Coughanowr; one of the two guards carried the tray in to him, and at that time he was seated at his desk, hard at work. Coughanowr's story is that the door between his office and Sir Henry's remained closed the entire time, and that he heard nothing to cause him to imagine a theft was being committed."

Owen Barham had lifted his gaze up to a painting of Mumbles Lighthouse that was hanging over the Chief Constable's desk, and was silent for so long that Snow said waspishly, "Well? I suppose you have all the answers ready for us now?"

"Oh, no," Barham replied, blinking vacantly behind his spectacles. "No, I haven't come to any firm conclusions. If it's at all possible, I'd prefer to see the third floor of Penryn House for myself, and talk to the men involved."

Snow was on the verge of objecting, but the Chief Constable held up a broad hand.

"Why not?" he asked, of no one in particular. "We've gone this far with the matter. Chief Inspector Jones, you take this young man along to Penryn House, and anywhere else he wants to visit. Meanwhile Inspector Sedlock and I will concentrate on other avenues of investigation. Jones, I expect a full report from you the instant anything of significance is uncovered."

From the station on Orchard Street it was no great distance at all, and the two struck out on foot, with the chief inspector setting a brisk pace despite his pudgy frame. They made their way south and over to the High Street, while a steady stream of omnibuses and the occasional motorcar puttered past.

As they walked Barham asked, tentatively, "Is it true what I've heard, that some Welshmen have strong feelings against the English?"

"It is," Jones said carefully, "but that's something as old as time itself. There're reactionaries everywhere these days, of course, but to be honest most folk here simply want the freedom to be Welsh, and not to be made to dress up in someone else's clothes. Do you know they won't even teach our children Welsh in the schools? But we're making steps; little by little, we're making steps."

"Could that be a motive behind this crime, to gain foreign support for the Welsh cause?"

Jones glanced at him, surprised. "Did you think, because of his last name–? Oh, no, lad, David Coughanowr's no more Welsh than you are. As far as Inspector Sedlock's men can tell, his family moved to England from Bavaria sometime in the last hundred years. Whether or not that means anything, I don't know."

At the very bottom of the High Street, on the western corner, just as the lane narrowed and became Castle Bailey Street, sat Penryn House. It was a venerable old pile, of pale blocks of stone that had darkened and spotted with time, and unlike its neighbours it sat back from the street, behind a walled-in courtyard.

They crossed the paving stones and were admitted by the commissionaire in his braided uniform and shining cap, and then climbed up the wide stairs to the third floor, to be met by the two Royal Marines on duty, with their navy-blue uniforms and flat-topped hats. By Owen Barham's request one of them showed the pair the little alcove with its table and register, and its thick curtain that allowed the gentlemen some measure of privacy whilst being inspected.

Barham turned the pages of the register back to the day of the theft, and saw that it reflected exactly what he had been told by Mr. Snow. Lord R- had visited in the morning; Mr. Griffiths and Colonel Vaughan had signed out at 11.48 and in again at 12.50; Sir Henry had signed out at 12.03

and back in at 1.00; Mr. Teal had signed out at 12.09 and back in at 12.58; and Mr. Coughanowr had not signed out at all until the end of the day.

They stepped around the corner and Jones rapped on the door of Sir Henry Cathcart's office. Sir Henry was a small man, nattily dressed, with receding dark hair and a harassed expression. He ushered them into his office and closed the door quietly behind them.

"It was too much to hope that you had good news, I suppose, Chief Inspector," he said sadly when Jones had explained the purpose of their visit. "I have my staff working as quickly as possible to reconstruct the missing design, without which we cannot continue, and at the same time, until this matter has been brought to some clear conclusion, I hardly feel justified in allowing young Coughanowr to handle anything more than the most minor duties… But don't let me hold you up. Whatever information I can provide I will, no matter how many times you need to ask it of me."

"Thank you, sir," Owen Barham said gratefully. "I'm simply trying to get as full a picture as I can of the circumstances involved. Is this the safe from which the paper was taken?"

"Yes, that's right."

The safe was small and black, with gold paint along its edges and gold lettering naming a local firm, and had been arranged so that it faced the Undersecretary's chair. He stood aside as the young man knelt behind his desk to examine it. It was operated by a single key, and had no other locking mechanism.

"How many people have keys to this safe?"

"Only myself. I had it specially installed here in my office when I arrived in Swansea to head this enterprise, and I've never had occasion to have extra keys made. Of course, they'll have a spare set on hand at the manufacturer's, in Wassail Street, but only you can say if that has any bearing on the matter."

"I'm certainly no expert on the subject," Barham continued, "but I can't see any scratches or obvious marks to indicate that the lock was forced."

"No," Jones said, "far as we know the mechanism wasn't tampered with."

Barham rose to his feet and stepped out from behind the Undersecretary's desk. "Have you ever misplaced the safe key, to your knowledge, even for a short time?" he asked.

"No."

"Do you keep it in any particular location?"

Sir Henry lifted a small ring of keys from his right-hand waistcoat pocket. "Right here, along with all of the other keys in my possession."

"Do you have any theory as to how the thief was able to open the safe in your absence?"

Sir Henry returned the keyring to his pocket with a despairing gesture. "If you can tell me that, I should be only too glad to listen. As for myself, I have no theories. It all seems quite incredible."

"There was mention of your noticing that your umbrella was wet when you returned to your office on the day of the theft. Could you explain the significance of that point to me?"

Sir Henry opened the door to his office and gestured into the corridor. Just outside his door, immediately around the corner from the guards' alcove, a square umbrella stand made of brass had been placed, and in it rested several umbrellas, most of them of the slim, tightly-furled type that could be found clutched in the hands of City bankers and politicians. One was larger than the rest, brown where they were black, and the red wood of its handle had been carved into a fiercely glowering dragon's head.

"The large one with the dragon handle is mine," Sir Henry explained. "A gift from my wife upon our arrival at our temporary quarters here in Swansea. A bit extravagant, no doubt, but I take pride in it, for a number of reasons. As it happens, young Coughanowr had left his lodgings in a hurry on the morning in question, forgetting his own umbrella, and as it was pouring down rain all that day I took pity on him and assured him he could borrow mine until the next day. Naturally, upon returning to this floor and seeing it spotted with water, I immediately concluded that he had heeded my suggestion. You can only imagine my feelings when it later became clear what were the circumstances under which he had done so...!"

"Had you had any previous problems with him, or misgivings on his account?"

"None, which makes all this the more confounding. Up to this point, I would have described him as a dedicated, industrious young man, with the potential to go very far indeed in Government service. Now, however..."

Barham had no other questions for Sir Henry Cathcart, and Jones asked him if he wished to see any of the various rooms on the third floor for himself. The young man shook his head.

"No," he said humbly, "I have full confidence in Inspector Sedlock when he says that he and his men made a thorough search of the building. I'm hardly likely to conceive of any hiding places they would have overlooked. I suppose I should speak to Mr. Coughanowr, though."

Their conversation with the man under suspicion was brief. David Coughanowr, just as he had when he was questioned by Inspector Sedlock, claimed to have no knowledge of the missing paper and no conception of how it could have been taken from Sir Henry's safe. He swore to them that he was innocent of any involvement in the affair, and as eager for the return of the stolen blueprint as any man in Penryn House.

They submitted to the necessary inspection before they departed the third floor, piling their belongings on the little table in the curtained alcove and unbuttoning their upper garments in turn for the guard's probing hands. Afterward, as they went down the stairs, Barham said, "I do have one other person I would like to question, one whom no one so far has mentioned questioning–the commissionaire."

Jones stared at him with a mixture of surprise and inquiry, but assented. They found the commissionaire inside his glass-fronted lodge, his cap on a table and his feet on a small stool, alert with both eyes and ears for a sign that he might be required. With his head bare he looked a great deal like the chief inspector, similar enough to be taken for his brother. Both men had round bellies, curly dark hair, and coal-black eyes that could be humorous one moment or shiningly shrewd the next–the very picture of storybook Welshmen, in fact. He scooped up his cap and settled it on his head at Jones's knock, but did not rise from his seat.

"So you've still not found the missing paper, Chief Inspector?"

"It's that obvious, is it, Davies?" returned Jones drily. "No, we're still on the hunt."

"I've heard it said none of the men on the third floor could've taken it. Maybe it was the *Tylwyth Teg* were responsible."

"The fairies," Jones muttered in explanation, at Owen Barham's inquiring glance.

"Were you on duty the day of the theft?" the young man asked. "It would have been a week ago today."

"Yes, I surely was. I remember it clear. It rained down buckets all that day long–old ladies and sticks, as my dear Grandad would've said."

Barham nodded. "From what I've been told, none of the men from the third floor, with one puzzling exception, set foot outside Penryn House that day. I imagine the main entranceway here is not the only way out of the building. How many others are there?"

"There's one other, a back way out through the kitchen into a narrow court, and a passage that'll eventually bring you into Goat Street–but you may take it from me, young sir, no fine Government gentleman like the ones you'll find at Penryn House would be caught dead in the muck and grime of that passage."

"If that's true, then, the thief must have walked past you at some point. Do you recall David Coughanowr passing your lodge between noon and one o'clock?"

The commissionaire rolled his shoulders in a gesture halfway between a shrug and a chuckle. "Sorry I am to disappoint you, young sir, but the only man from the third floor I saw go out was Mr. Teal –and that was just to make a 'phone call."

"Oh? You could make out clearly what he did?"

"Oh, yes. You see how the front of my lodge bellies out a good bit, past the entranceway? It gives me a fine view of everything happening in the street–especially on a day like that one, when the squalls were driving everyone to shelter. Yes, Mr. Teal went straight down to the telephone box on the corner, made a quick connexion, and was back again in no time at all."

Owen Barham, lifting his eyes placidly to the window, said, "I'm afraid I don't understand. Is Penryn House not on the exchange?"

"Oh, yes," Davies answered, "we have telephone cabinets here, just outside the dining hall, but for trunk calls–and personal calls they'd rather not risk having interrupted–the gentlemen use the box on the street corner."

"Perhaps the telephones here were all in use at the time," suggested Jones.

"Well," the commissionaire said with slow humour, "seeing as how he already had his hat and overcoat and umbrella when he come down from the third floor, I'd say that probably wasn't the reason. And now that I come to recollect it, that wasn't the only odd thing about that telephone call. Would you think it, he was in such a hurry to make his call that he didn't even open his umbrella on the way to the corner, only using it on the way back? There's a lesson there in not being in haste, gentlemen, for it only leads to discomfort–him having to endure the rain pouring down on his head while having such a fine large umbrella to hand…"

Barham's gaze snapped to the man's round, ruddy face. "Tell me," he asked, "did you see anyone use the telephone box after Mr. Teal?"

"Well, yes, I did. Only a tramp, it was, but he claimed the box immediately Mr. Teal'd finished making his call."

"Can you describe him?"

"If you like," the commissionaire said placidly, and proceeded to amaze his audience with his powers of recollection. "He was no more than medium height and weight, and probably in his middle age, since he had a limp and a bit of a stoop, and a thick black beard to the middle of his chest. He was wearing a long, ragged coat and an old hat pushed down over his ears, and clutching a worn grip in one hand."

Barham listened carefully, and then nodded and asked, "Do you have a pen and paper?"

"I've a bit of paper and a stub of pencil here in a drawer, young sir, but there's a writing desk in the lobby for the gentlemen's use, and it'll have everything you could possibly want."

The young man nodded again and disappeared past the chief inspector into the corridor, returning a minute or two later with a half-sheet of fine notepaper covered with several lines of clear, admirable penmanship.

"If you'll give this to Inspector Sedlock," he told Jones, "it will indicate to him the most promising line of inquiry. I've written it out as best I could. I must leave now, and try to catch up with the rest of my class. I've missed a good portion of the lecture tour already this morning."

Jones glanced over the sheet of notepaper. "But–"

"It's been a pleasure working with you, Chief Inspector," the young man said, shaking his hand. "I really must go. If I hurry, I believe I can meet the others at St. Mary's."

He went quickly out, and was shortly after seen making his way up the street, signalling for an omnibus, while the two Welshmen stared at each other in bemusement.

Two days later, in the afternoon, there was another gathering in the office of the Chief Constable. On this occasion the number of those present was greater than before: in addition to the Chief Constable, Inspector Sedlock, Chief Inspector Jones, and Mr. Snow, the head of the naval engineering venture, Sir Henry Cathcart, was in attendance; and by means of a telephone extension that had been brought in, connecting them with his lodgings in Torrington Square, Bloomsbury, so was Owen Barham.

On the desk in front of them lay a large square of thin paper covered with lines and notations, and absolutely meaningless to any of them save Sir Henry: the recovered blueprint.

"It's wonderful, gentlemen, absolutely wonderful," he said enthusiastically. "To have this back again, and to know that our undertaking will be able to proceed on schedule… You are all to be commended."

"To give credit where it's due," said Inspector Sedlock, "it was young Mr. Barham's suggestion that led to our finding the lost paper. I suppose, as a starting point, I may as well read to you the note he penned for me after his visit to Penryn House."

He took a crumpled half-sheet of notepaper from his pocket and read the following:

> *"Does Bradley Teal have a friend or acquaintance of the following description: young and fair-haired, clean-shaven and perhaps athletic? Is it possible this man was in Swansea on the day of the*

*theft? If the answer to both questions is yes, the missing paper will be found in the possession of one of the two men."*

Sir Henry sat back in his chair. "Bradley Teal? Then the thief is not–"

"David Coughanowr? No, he had nothing to do with it."

"I don't understand," Sir Henry said. "I don't understand at all. We agreed that it was impossible for anyone other than young Coughanowr to have taken the paper–and really, it seemed impossible that even he could have done so–and now you're saying that another of my staff is the guilty party?"

"Exactly, Sir Henry," replied Sedlock. "Perhaps it would be best if we allowed Mr. Barham to explain his reasoning. That may make everything a good bit clearer."

Barham cleared his throat, and his voice issued tinnily from the telephone receiver in the centre of the Chief Constable's desk.

"Yes. Well, I will admit that after the fundamental situation was explained to me my mind was in something of a muddle, and even more so after I was shown the security precautions on the third floor of Penryn House. It seemed very much as though the crime were impossible, as Sir Henry said. The first conjecture that occurred to me was the famous one put forth by Poe in his 'Purloined Letter,' that the stolen paper might be hidden in such an obvious location that no one thought to look for it there, but I quickly disregarded that notion. I could not imagine that two thorough searches, by Sir Henry's staff and again by Inspector Sedlock and his men, would have failed to uncover the paper, wherever it might have been hidden.

"But how could the paper have been carried away from the third floor? The guards, who had been thoroughly vetted and found to be trustworthy, had searched every man who left that floor around the time of the theft–and David Coughanowr, by all the available evidence, had never even left the floor. The only way that made sense was in some sort of package, for if it had been secreted anywhere on the thief's person it would have been discovered without delay.

"And yet the rules at Penryn House prohibit the third-floor staff from leaving with anything that could conceivably contain Government papers.

"It wasn't until Chief Inspector Jones and I spoke with the commissionaire at Penryn House that I understood the only way the crime could have been committed, and how the thief had taken the paper out right under the guards' noses.

"As soon as you left the third floor that day, Sir Henry, the thief stepped across the corridor to your office, taking an umbrella from the stand outside your door as he did so. All of the steps I'm about to relate, were, I'm sure, worked out far in advance of the crime. He unlocked the safe with a duplicate key, and taking the desired paper from it he *wound the paper around the shaft of the umbrella.* It was as safe as a babe in a cradle there: with the umbrella closed there was nothing to indicate its presence, and in the unlikely event it was discovered, he only had to explain that he'd picked up the wrong umbrella by mistake, and suspicion would immediately have shifted to the umbrella's owner–or to the person to whom he'd loaned the umbrella that day. The thief then left your office and submitted cheerfully to a search by the guards, who very likely never gave the umbrella a second glance.

"When he reached the first floor of Penryn House the thief made his way down the street on the pretext of making a telephone call, and left the stolen paper to be collected by his confederate, who was disguised as a tramp."

"Ah, the tramp," murmured Chief Inspector Jones.

"The crime was cleverly planned," Barham continued. "It was only the commissionaire's description of the umbrella Mr. Teal was carrying when he made his 'telephone call' that gave me the elucidating clue. He said it was 'a fine large umbrella'–besides mentioning that Mr. Teal didn't open it until he reached the 'phone box, despite the pouring rain–and only one umbrella in the third-floor stand could be described that way, Sir Henry–yours.

"I therefore left a note for Inspector Sedlock describing the likely appearance of Mr. Teal's confederate, and suggesting that the missing paper was in the possession of one of the two men."

"I see the description of the confederate," interjected Jones, "sounds nothing like the tramp that Davies, the commissionaire, saw. Did you simply reverse every physical detail that he gave you to come up with that description?"

"Yes, sir," said the voice from the receiver. "I assumed the second man had cobbled together a disguise that was the opposite of his real appearance, as most not particularly imaginative people would, and proceeded from there."

"The description Mr. Barham gave me," said Sedlock, taking up the story, "fit Teal's cousin, a young man named Guy Entwhistle-Endicott, exactly. He has a small estate outside Highbury, and late yesterday evening the missing paper was discovered in a locked desk in his study there. He and Bradley Teal have since been taken into charge, and will face trial for violating the Official Secrets Act–in a closed session, of course."

"But how," objected Sir Henry, "did Teal gain access to my safe? To my knowledge I have the only key there is to it–unless he somehow stole the master keys from the manufacturer's office?"

"No, he had recourse to another method," Inspector Sedlock answered, and took from one pocket a small wooden box, only slightly larger than a matchbox, with a hinged lid. He placed the box on the corner of the Chief Constable's desk and opened it so that all could see the two squares of greyish-brown matter inside. "He used this little toy, which contains artist's clay. Takes a good, firm impression, one that a none-too-scrupulous locksmith could use to make a duplicate key. It's a very old thief's dodge. We found this hidden in a drawer in his home in Kensington; apparently he felt he might have use for it again in the future."

"On some previous occasion, while the two of you were in the alcove on the third floor waiting to be searched," added Owen Barham, "Mr. Teal took the opportunity to make an impression of your safe key. The alcove, as you know, Sir Henry, has only a single small table for the gentlemen to place their belongings on, and only one of the two guards performs the searches at a given time. It would have taken merely a moment for him to step over to the table, while you and the guard were otherwise occupied, and use his device. Then, having a copy of the safe key, he could plan the other steps of the theft at his leisure."

Sir Henry shook his head, and rising, placed the recovered paper in the briefcase he had brought, locking it securely. "Gentlemen, I cannot thank you enough for your work in this matter. You have rendered your country a fine service, and guaranteed our continued naval security in the future. You certainly have my gratitude."

He shook hands all around and took his leave, accompanied by Mr. Snow. As they reached the doorway he paused.

"About the boy who assisted in recovering this paper–" he said in a low voice, "surely Downing Street, and the Admiralty, might see their way to presenting him with some small token of appreciation? The circumstances, of course, hardly lend themselves to any public gesture…"

"I'll see what can be done," Snow replied austerely.

Some little time later a messenger arrived at Owen Barham's room in Torrington Square, and the package he left was found to contain an elegant fountain pen set in silver and cherry wood, along with a plain envelope devoid of any superscription whatsoever, inside of which was a note reading simply, "With the esteem of His Majesty's Government." On the cover of the set, stained a deeper red, was an engraved outline of the ancient dragon of Wales.

# THE VANISHING OF VALDONATO

Liidia Peetre

Prudence Patience sighed vexedly and thrust the pages of the newspaper together with some force. "Oh, why can't they find any answers? I'm sorry, Mrs. Birdseye."

Her landlady, whose penny had paid for the journal, tsk-tsked indulgently and reassembled it with care. Miss Patience's roommate, Gertrude Frumm, said around a mouthful of toast and marmalade, "No progress in the case, love?"

"Not a single step that I can tell. At this rate we'll be besieged by reporters until Doomsday."

They were seated around the little table in the back parlour of Mrs. Birdseye's boardinghouse in Bethnal Green, having a quick breakfast before the younger women departed for their respective workplaces. Roughly a week and a half earlier the head of Miss Patience's firm had disappeared from his office in the middle of the morning, under baffling circumstances, taking with him a quarter of a million pounds in company funds. With the discovery of his dead body in the Thames a few days afterward the mystery only deepened, and with their access to the company itself being firmly barred, the representatives of the press had taken to flocking around those few people who were the last to see him alive–among them being Miss Patience.

"Pru," said Miss Frumm, "I had an idea come to me in the night. You know my brother works as a porter at University College? He says there's a young gentleman there, one of the students, who's gathered a bit of a reputation as a Sherlock. Why don't we tell him the story, and see if he can make anything of it? What I mean is, if the police can't seem to find any clues, why shouldn't we find someone who can?"

Miss Patience finished off the last of her kippers and reached for the teapot. "It can't do any harm, I suppose. All right, Gertie, I'm game."

As the two young women clattered down the boardinghouse's front steps, waving off the handful of reporters that came surging forward and peering about for a respectable-looking bus, Miss Frumm said, "Chin up, Pru! Just wait 'til you meet this wonder detective. You'll see."

"I look forward to it with bated breath," her friend responded pertly.

That evening a group gathered in the front parlour of Mrs. Birdseye's boardinghouse. Apart from Miss Patience and Miss Frumm, those present included Bertram Frumm, who shared with his sister mousy brown hair and a pugnacious nose; a darkly Irish youth named Jimmy Clough; and the guest of honour, Owen Barham. Miss Patience examined the latter discreetly and was not necessarily impressed: he certainly looked like the student he was, with his brushed-back blond hair and light blue eyes looking out from behind round spectacles, but he could hardly be a day over twenty, half a decade younger than her, and his slightly vacant expression did not spell Master Detective to her.

"Well, sis," said Frumm, as Mrs. Birdseye trundled around providing them all with cups of tea and biscuits, "here we are, as promised. What's the flap all about?"

"You hush, Bertie Frumm," responded his sibling. "We're not here to hear you. Pru's going to tell us the whole story, and we're hoping maybe Mr. Barham can shed some light on what really happened. Go on, Pru."

Miss Patience cleared her throat a trifle self-consciously as their eyes turned to her. "I work as a typist for the firm of Huntingdon and Ffolliott, Limited. It's a mercantile concern in the City, in Copthall Court, with holdings all round the world, from Shanghai to Rio de Janeiro. Mssrs. Huntingdon and Ffolliott are long gone; the head of the firm–at least until last week–was a man named Immanuel Valdonato. Mr. Fairhope, who worked directly under Mr. Valdonato, asked me to come in to the office on Saturday the 15th, as there were some urgent reports needed typed up, and the work couldn't wait until Monday. When I got to the top floor, where Mr. Valdonato's office was, I found that I was the only typist there. There was only one other person in sight, apart from Mr. Fairhope and Mr. Valdonato, a painter working in some empty offices next door.

"At first everything proceeded normally. Mr. Valdonato came in, bid me good morning, and went on through into his office. Mr. Fairhope was already there when I arrived, in the outer office. He'd warned me that he'd be in and out of the office throughout the morning, and Mr. Valdonato would want someone near at hand for any secretarial work that was needed, which was only reasonable. Mr. Fairhope was quite right; he came and went several times, but I was busy with the typing work he gave me and didn't think anything of it.

"Finally, at around eleven o'clock, he came in, went into his office and through into Mr. Valdonato's office, and came right back out again. 'Miss Patience,' he said, 'where's Mr. Valdonato?'

"I didn't know what to say to that. Mr. Valdonato hadn't left his office all morning. He had to still be in there, but when I said so, Mr. Fairhope responded, 'Come and see for yourself.'

"I left my desk and he took me through into the inner office. It was empty. Mr. Valdonato's chair stood back a little from his desk, as though he'd just gotten up, but he was nowhere in sight. Mr. Fairhope strode over to a door on the right side of the room and opened it; it turned out to be the door to a cramped washroom, but there was no one in it. Then he crossed to the door on the left side of the room. This connected with the neighbouring suite of offices, which were being painted, like I said.

" 'Here, you,' Mr. Fairhope said to the painter, 'has anyone passed through here in the last thirty minutes?'

"The painter came to the door and shook his head. 'No, guv'nor,' he said, 'I haven't seen a soul all morning.' I went over to the door myself and looked past the man into the other room–I couldn't help myself–and the only things in it were some cans of paint, ladders, and sheets. There was no place in that room for anyone to hide, just as there was no place in Mr. Valdonato's office for him to hide. And why on earth would he have been hiding from us, anyway?

"At that Mr. Fairhope said the only thing to do was to summon the police, and he sent me down to the street to find a constable. I eventually found one, about a block away, and explained the situation to him, and he came back with me and searched every inch of those offices. The constable didn't find any sign of Mr. Valdonato, apart from a bit of broken watch chain under his desk, and he told the three of us to stay where we were, and he went downstairs to telephone for an inspector. When the inspector came the two of them searched the offices again, with the same result. The only other thing they found was that a quarter of a million pounds in registered bonds were missing from the safe behind Mr. Valdonato's desk.

"After all that Mr. Fairhope said there was no point in my staying any longer, and he sent me home. When we all came in to work on the following Monday Mr. Valdonato was still missing, and Mr. Fairhope and the other directors had to have a meeting about what to do. They sent us away, telling us not to come back until after lunch.

"That evening the newspaper carried the news that Mr. Valdonato'd put in an appearance at his bank that morning, with the missing bonds, and had them converted to cash– and then drove away to parts unknown.

"Then, the next evening, Mr. Valdonato's body was pulled out of the Thames. Apparently he'd been strangled to death. The police are still searching for the money he took, as well as any clues to his killer, but so far they haven't found a thing.

"I–we–thought after hearing the whole story, you might be able to provide some answers as to how he disappeared from his office, or at least some possibilities." Miss Patience gave a little laugh and a quick shake of her raven locks. "Honestly, Mr. Barham, I don't expect you to tell us who killed Mr. Valdonato–that's the business of the police. I just want to give the reporters someone else to plague for a change."

Barham nodded vaguely and asked, "I presume it isn't unusual for you to be called in to work on a Saturday?"

"No, it happens all the time. Usually, as I said, it's to finish up reports that can't wait until the next business day."

"But it was Mr. Fairhope who asked you to come in, and not Mr. Valdonato?"

"Oh, no. Mr. Valdonato didn't deal directly with us girls in the typing pool. Our instructions always came from Mr. Fairhope or one of the other directors."

"Is it usual for you to be the only typist present?"

"I don't know that I was the only one, necessarily. The main typing room is on another floor, you see, and that day I went straight up to the top floor, as I'd been told to do, without stopping to natter with anyone. The other girls might've been at their desks, every one, for all I know."

"How did Mr. Valdonato seem that morning? Preoccupied, or worried, or anything of that sort?"

"He seemed his normal, distantly friendly self. He said, '*Buongiorno*, miss,' as he passed by, with a faint smile, and in that heavy accent of his. Of course I didn't expect him to remember my name."

"You mentioned the discovery of the missing bonds. Was the safe in the inner office standing open, then?"

"Oh, no. The inspector, after they'd searched all over for the second time, had Mr. Fairhope look through Mr. Valdonato's desk to determine if anything was missing, and the safe as well. Mr. Fairhope, since he worked so closely with Mr. Valdonato, knows the combination to the safe by heart."

After a brief pause, which led the others to expect some definitive pronouncement, the young man said merely: "I'd like very much to see the office in question. Do you think that might be possible?"

Miss Patience knit her brow and pressed her mouth together in an uncertain frown. The others immediately began to chivvy her.

"Come on, Pru, love," said Miss Frumm. "We want to get to the bottom of this, don't we?"

Miss Patience relented. "All right. I'll see what I can do. Meet me at the entrance to Copthall Court at six tomorrow evening, and I'll signal if everything is clear."

At the appointed hour Miss Patience emerged from the front doors of her firm to find at the far end of the court, not merely Owen Barham, but all four of them. She waved at them to come forward and shook her head in disbelief when the group reached her.

"What on earth are you all doing here?" she asked in an undertone, not wanting the doorman to overhear.

Miss Frumm put her head close to her friend's with a wide-eyed, conspiratorial grin. "It's really very simple, isn't it, m'dear? We all want to know the answer to this mystery."

"If you'd set the time any sooner," added her brother with what he imagined was a roguish smirk, "you'd've had to do without me. But as it is, I managed to slip away from work early, and here we are."

"Yes, here we are," echoed his sister, rolling her eyes. "Well, Pru, can we go up and have a look at this magician's cabinet of yours?"

"Yes, Mr. Fairhope and the other directors are gone now. Follow me, all of you, and let me do any talking that's required. And for goodness' sake try and act as though you belong here!"

They trooped inside past the doorman, who tipped his hat with a questioning look but said nothing. Once in the lift Miss Patience instructed the operator, a lad of sixteen or so who was growing a pencil moustache in imitation of some sheik of filmdom, to take them all the way to the top.

"Bit late for a visit to the office, isn't it, miss?" he inquired cheerily.

"Students from University College for a tour, Freddie," Miss Patience said with a confidence she didn't quite feel. "We didn't want to disturb the directors while they were working."

At the top floor she led the others down the hallway and into the rooms where the events of the 15th had occurred. The outermost room was the largest, with four desks–or tables, more accurately–arranged in two rows, and another pair of desks off to one side. The former were equipped with typewriters and the other accoutrements of clerical work, and faced, across a small corridor that ran off to the left, a door with a frosted glass window.

"That's the door to Mr. Fairhope's office," said Miss Patience, "or what was Mr. Fairhope's office. He's since taken over Mr. Valdonato's office."

She opened the door and they passed into the outer office. It contained a desk of black walnut and a padded chair on the left, assorted cabinets and chairs for clients, and in the right corner a small desk similar to the ones outside, with space atop it where a typewriter could have been placed.

Barham gestured toward it. "Is this where Mr. Fairhope had you do your work on that Saturday morning?"

Miss Patience shook her head. "Oh, no, at one of the desks in the other room."

He looked thoughtful and opened the door to the inner office, which also had a frosted glass window in it, one that had been recently repainted with the words "N. Fairhope." This office contained a heavy oaken desk, larger than the one in the outer office, and the padded chair that accompanied it was more ornate. A pair of filing cabinets took up the far corners, one holding a bust of Napoleon Bonaparte, while a compact black safe sat directly behind the desk, beneath the single window. A pair of chairs for visitors completed the furnishings.

Barham first stepped to the door on the right, which opened, as Miss Patience had said, onto a small washroom. The washroom had a tiny window, barely the size of a shoebox, and no other exit.

He closed the washroom door and went to the window behind the desk. It was not much larger than the other; if it had been utterly necessary, he imagined, he could have wriggled out through it. He swung open the window, and stood on his tiptoes to thrust his head through the opening.

In one of those incongruous situations that occur in great metropolises such as London, the back side of Copthall Court, that gallery of staid and dignified counting houses, was a dismal lane bearing the inapposite name of Angel Court. It was a narrow passage, hardly more than an alley, lined with sagging, soot-begrimed tenements, and as Barham looked down its length three urchins in ragged, dirty costumes returned his stare boldly.

He closed the window and asked, "What sort of build did Mr. Valdonato have? Do you think he could have squeezed through this window?"

Miss Patience gave a startled laugh. "Oh, no, it's impossible! Mr. Valdonato, bless his soul, was short and round. There's no way he could ever have fit through there."

"What about Mr. Fairhope?"

"No, not him, either. He's tall and broad-shouldered, and I suppose you could say handsome, in a way…" She trailed off in faint embarrassment.

Barham crossed to the other door, on the left side of the office, and opened it to peer into the adjoining offices. The painting work had since been finished there, the walls gleaming a crisp white, but as yet only a few large pieces of furniture had been moved in.

"Can you tell me about the painter that was here that day? What was he like?"

Miss Patience shrugged. "What's to tell? He was short and spindly, dressed in one of those one-piece suits painters normally wear. He had a full head of curly red hair under his cap. And, if I'm being honest, there was something familiar about his face, but I haven't been able to think what it was…"

"And he was working alone?"

"Yes, that's right."

Barham closed the connecting door and returned to the large outer room with Miss Patience, the others close behind. He gestured toward the desks.

"Where exactly were you sitting on that Saturday morning?" he asked.

"Mr. Fairhope had me sit here, at this first seat."

The typing tables were long enough that two individuals could share one. Miss Patience indicated a wooden chair at one of the foremost tables, on the inner side, almost directly in front of the door to Fairhope's former office. Barham sat down in the chair and looked around. From that seat he had a clear view of the door before him, as well as the entrance to the suite of offices beside it, and with a minimum of effort he could even see the next door past that one.

"Where does this hallway lead?"

"It connects with another hallway that runs back to the rear stairs, the only other way off this floor."

Owen Barham's expression grew more thoughtful, and the rest of them regarded him in anticipation. His friend Jimmy Clough said, "Have you got it now, boyo? The answer to the whole disappearin' act?"

Barham nodded, almost dismissively, but they were once more destined to be disappointed. Instead of launching into an explanation, or even hinting at one, he said, "I think it would be a good idea to bring in a private enquiry agent at this point."

Miss Patience's dark eyes flashed in consternation. "After all this," she cried, "you want me to find someone else to investigate for me? I can't afford to hire a detective! I thought you were going to solve this mystery!"

"Now, now, half a mo' ," responded Bertie Frumm soothingly. "Don't panic, love. How much can it really be? Maybe if we all pitch in… That is," he asked Barham, "if you're sure a detective really is necessary?"

Barham nodded again, and said apologetically, "There are facts I'd like to learn, and I can't envision any other way of accomplishing that task. I doubt very much the police will be inclined to discuss the case with any of us."

It was a fair point, one none of them could muster an argument against. The ensuing discussion ended with the decision that, since it was his suggestion, Owen Barham would be the one responsible for finding an investigator willing to help, and the question of funds would be tabled until he had spoken to such an investigator and gotten some concrete details.

A few days passed before he found himself, one early evening, in an upstairs office in Whitefriars Street, in a block of small shops and modest commercial firms. The man behind the somewhat worn desk, Thomas Beauclerk Silver by name, was about ten years his senior, with a narrow face capped by medium brown hair and dark eyes that managed to seem both intelligent and kind.

He listened to Barham's story without interruption, puffing on a long clay pipe, and at the end of it said, "Hm. The Valdonato case, eh? I've been following it in the papers. The police are at an impasse, Barings Bank has become desperate enough to offer a reward for recovery of the stolen money, and you think you have the explanation to the whole thing?"

"I have a hypothesis," Barham replied with quiet dignity. "More facts would be required to come to a definite conclusion. That's why I've come to you, for you to dig up those facts for us."

"You're certain you and your friends can afford it? My rates are seventy pounds a day plus expenses, and there's no telling how long it could take to learn whatever it is you're wanting to learn... Tell you what," Silver said abruptly, "I'll make a bargain with you. If what I discover leads to the stolen money being found, I'll waive my usual fee. Does that strike you as a fair offer?"

"Generous, in fact," said Barham.

Silver smiled briefly, and took up a pen and notebook. "Good. Now, what exactly do you want me to find out for you?"

Owen Barham listed the points on which he desired more information, and Silver jotted them down in his own style of shorthand. "I see," he said at the end. "You truly do have a hypothesis, don't you? I'll start to work on this first thing in the morning, and let you know what develops."

It was the late afternoon of the following day when he called at the student lodgings in Torrington Square, with the same notebook in his pocket, ready to give the initial report to his young client.

"Immanuel Valdonato, sixty-one years of age, a widower. He emigrated to London about twenty years ago, after the death of his wife, bringing with him two servants from his village of Gattinara, in northern Italy. Acquired stock in Huntingdon and Ffolliott, Ltd., and quickly rose to become head of the firm. No complaints against him from his associates in industry or his neighbours in Holborn.

"Neil Fairhope, forty-two years of age, bachelor. Worked directly under Mr. Valdonato at Huntingdon and Ffolliott for the past eight years. Lives in a little villa in Knightsbridge, and likewise has no complaints from his neighbours, though he is known to invest heavily in the horses and at the roulette table.

"I could give you some specifics on the other directors of the firm, but it's been established beyond doubt that none of them were present on the morning of the 15th.

"The police, as you suspected, did not question any inhabitants of Angel Court at the time of the disappearance, though the firm's back entrance is in that street. There's a tanner's shop at the end of the court, and it just so happens three lads from the shop were taking a respite and sharing a cigaret round the time when the disappearance occurred. They said at that time, a few minutes after eleven o'clock so far as they could recall, they witnessed a pair of painters emerge from the building carrying a bundle of old rags and refuse bound to a ladder by ropes. It seems it was a fairly heavy load, by the trouble they took with it. The two men stowed it into the back of a lorry parked nearby and re-entered the building, and that was the last our apprentices knew of the matter, since they had to return to their work as well."

"How did they describe these two painters?" asked Barham.

"One was small and red-headed, they agreed, and the other was tall and broad-shouldered. The first matches the description of the painter seen by Miss Patience, who gave his name as Albert Brown when questioned by the police. He also gave a spurious address, and has not been seen since–and his fellow painter seems to have vanished before the police ever arrived on the scene. Are we dealing with a rash of disappearances now?" Owen Barham raised his pale eyebrows, and Silver grinned. "Don't tell me, you have a hypothesis.

"The police puzzled over the businessman's vanishing act all week-end, and then promptly forgot about it in the face of subsequent events. On that Monday morning a few minutes past ten o'clock, just after it opened for the day, Immanuel Valdonato entered his bank and presented the missing bonds to be realised. These were registered in his name, and he signed for the money in a shaky hand. He behaved unusually: he kept his hat low over his eyes, had a muffler wrapped round his throat and face, and spoke not one word the entire time. His chauffeur, who accompanied him inside, explained that his employer had lost his voice due to illness, and specified what he wanted, and the transaction was carried out accordingly. The clerk who assisted him said that he appeared ill, even as though he had lost a little weight, from the way he walked and the way his clothes fit."

"Did you get a description of the chauffeur?"

"The clerk said he was tall and well-built, with a strong Cockney accent. Begins to sound familiar, doesn't it? I should mention that Valdonato's own man, who acted as his valet and driver, is short and slight, and barely speaks any English. Did our missing painters kidnap Valdonato for his bonds, do you think?"

Barham did not reply to this, and Silver, who had spoken rhetorically, flipped to the next page of his notebook.

"That was the last anyone saw of Immanuel Valdonato until the next morning, at ten-forty-seven, when his body was pulled from the Thames at Wapping Old Stairs. From the medical examination afterward it appears he was strangled to death with a rope, of a common type that can be purchased at any of a thousand shops across the city. It seems his murderer had attempted to weigh the body down to prevent its discovery but had failed at this, and the body'd been damaged enough by contact with ships and boats that there wasn't much else definite the authorities could learn from it." Silver raised his head from his notebook and regarded his young client curiously. "Does all of that answer the questions you had?"

"It fits my hypothesis," Barham replied, "but there's more to be learned" –and he proceeded to give the detective another set of instructions. Silver narrowed his eyes at the specific nature of the inquiries and whistled tunelessly.

"So that's the way the wind is blowing, is it? Well, it'll take a bit longer to get results this time, especially with the week-end upon us. I was able to gather most of the facts you asked for the first time from the newspaper offices and from a friend I have in Scotland Yard, but these other points will take more doing. I'll keep you informed, though, not to worry."

As it turned out, Silver contacted his client on the following Monday, and at Barham's suggestion they called at Mrs. Birdseye's boardinghouse together, just after the conclusion of evening tea. They met with Miss Patience in the front parlour, while the landlady listened wide-eyed from a seat in the corner and tried to follow what she heard.

Silver, as before, took his well-thumbed notebook from his pocket, and began by presenting the latest set of facts to Barham. "There is a public house on the east side of Knightsbridge–in Holloway, speaking technically–called the Nag's Head, and one of its regulars is a man named Abel Denley, who appears to fit the description of the painter Miss Patience saw. He rooms with his sister and her husband, and I was able to obtain from them a photograph of him. Not a very recent one, but it's the best we can do, I'm afraid." He took a wallet from an inner pocket and extracted two photographs, the first of which he handed across to the young woman. "Would you tell us, miss, if this man looks familiar?"

Miss Patience stared at the picture for only the briefest moment, and then lifted her head eagerly. "That's him! That's the man, the one who was there the morning Mr. Valdonato disappeared."

"This Denley," Silver continued, "is not a painter by trade, but works at a glazier's in Basil Street. He appears to have come into some money of late, though not necessarily a quarter of a million pounds' worth. How about this photograph, miss?"

He handed her the other one. It was a copy of the first, and had been altered at the photographer's studio, obviously so once one knew what to look for. Weight had been added to the central figure, the cap on his head had been replaced by a more formal hat, and a muffler now encircled his throat and chin.

"It's rough work," Silver said apologetically, "but my friend was rather pressed for time…"

"But–" protested Miss Patience. "But it's Mr. Valdonato. What does this mean? Was he the painter in the empty offices? But that can't possibly be. There's no way he was masquerading as that little red-headed mite, not with his size."

"No," Barham agreed with a smile, "he wasn't. You're correct about that. What else, Mr. Silver?"

"The barman at the Nag's Head informed me that Neil Fairhope, or someone fitting his description, has frequented the pub in the past, but has been absent in recent days.

"I located a costumer's shop in Sedding Street that hired out two painter's outfits, one for a short man and one for a tall man, a chauffeur's outfit for a tall man, a double-breasted suit and hat for a short man along with padding to make the wearer appear heavier than he actually was, and a wig of woolly black hair. This would have been early in the week of the 15th. The hirer was a small red-headed man who called himself Alfred Smith, and said the articles were for a modest production being put on at the Royal Court Theatre, which is not very far from there. Needless to say the good people at the Royal Court have no knowledge of Mr. Smith or his costumes.

"As for your last point, Fairhope drove himself to the firm on the Monday following Valdonato's disappearing act, not typical behaviour for him, and he set the time of the company meeting at eleven o'clock, so as to have some sort of plan in effect for the rest of the day. From ten o'clock to eleven o'clock his whereabouts are unaccounted for.

"So," he concluded, watching Barham's face closely, "does this tell you what you wanted to know?"

"It all fits together," Barham said, answering the question Silver had not asked, "but it isn't proof, any of it. It might be corroborating evidence, but that would have to be determined by the Solicitor-General's Office."

"All we can do," the detective said, "is to pass the facts, and your explanation of them, on to my friend at the Yard. Perhaps they'll be able to make a case out of it all."

Barham leaned forward in his chair with his hands gripping his knees. "Or," he replied, "we could let him incriminate himself. Do you know the exact location of the villa in Knightsbridge? If we were to borrow a page from the master, specifically from 'A Scandal in Bohemia'…"

As he explained Miss Patience found herself joining her landlady in wonderment, and Silver's respect for his young client increased.

"It could very possibly work," he said. "It will take some arranging, though. I can telephone you when I've gotten everything in place—"

"What about tonight?" Barham asked bluntly. "I think it would be best to strike as soon as we can, before the men involved take fright and flee."

Silver saw from his client's determination that there was no point in further palaver. He and Barham bid the ladies good evening, and he deposited the young man back at his lodgings in Torrington Square and went off to tackle the necessary preparations.

A few minutes after midnight found a handful of individuals waiting in the shadowy corners of an otherwise empty lane in Kensington. A gibbous moon shone weakly through ribbons of cloud high above. It was only the midpoint of spring, and though the days were tolerable, once the sun disappeared beneath the earth the temperature plummeted with it, so that the watchers were huddled in their overcoats.

Thomas Silver drew from his pocket what appeared in the pale light to be two cylinders of heavy pasteboard, slightly longer than his hand, and exhibited them to Owen Barham. "The costumer in Sedding Street was able to get hold of these for me," he whispered. "They put out plumes of white smoke, not black, but in the dark that shouldn't make much difference."

He set off in the crêpe-soled shoes he had slipped on for the occasion, swung open the gate of the house opposite almost soundlessly, and disappeared inside. A short time later there was a very faint clatter, then after a brief interval another such sound, and presently he came into view at the front of the house again.

When he reached the front door he abandoned any effort to be quiet, and instead took the opposite tack. He pounded on the door, shouting at the top of his lungs, "Fire! Fire!"

He kept up this barrage until the door was opened by a drowsy-looking young man with somewhat disheveled hair, evidently a servant.

"Fire!" Silver gasped at him. "Come on, man, you've got to get out of there! I saw smoke coming from one of the back windows. Is there anyone else in the house? You must get everyone out!"

The young man, addled with sleep and the sudden alarm, whirled and rushed off toward the stairs leading to the second floor, leaving the front door yawning open. Silver retreated to the far side of the street and rejoined Owen Barham and his friend from Scotland Yard.

Silence returned to the lane. Silver was just beginning to doubt that their subterfuge had worked when two figures burst from the open front door of the villa, racing pell-mell for the street. The first was the servant, fumbling with the belt of his house coat. Behind him, carrying a weighty valise, with his open dressing gown flapping against his long legs, was his dark-haired, broad-shouldered employer. The pair got as far as the pavement before the stillness of the night struck them, the lack of flames and noise and commotion, and they stopped abruptly, almost colliding into one another.

Silver's friend from Scotland Yard stepped forward to meet them, joined by a second man bearing a lantern. "Just a moment, if you please, sir," he said, in that polite yet steely tone the English police have perfected over the ages. "We'll need to see what's in that bag, if you don't mind."

"What is this?" objected the man clutching the valise. "What's happening here? I don't know you gentlemen."

The second officer spoke up then, lifting his lantern higher. "You do know me, sir. Inspector Cotton. We've spoken before. Will you open the bag, Mr. Fairhope?"

"This valise contains confidential papers—"

The financier's protest drew no response from the stony-faced men before him. Fairhope, with the lantern glaring in his eyes, ground his teeth together and opened the valise. The two officers bent their heads forward and peered at the bundles of banknotes, still in their paper sleeves, that filled the bag.

Inspector Cotton gestured for his men to come forward. "Neil Fairhope," he said, "I arrest you on suspicion of the murder of Immanuel Valdonato…"

"And that," said Thomas Silver when later recounting the night's events, "was that. He had no proper explanation for why he was in possession of the money received from Valdonato's bank, and his valet quickly confessed that his employer had not returned to his home on that Monday morning, as he had previously stated for fear of losing his position. There went Fairhope's alibi, in one fell swoop."

They were gathered in a tea shop called the Lion several days afterward, Miss Patience and the entire group that had originally collected in Mrs. Birdseye's parlour, as well as Thomas Silver, puffing on his clay pipe. Miss Patience shook her head.

"So he forced Mr. Valdonato to change his bonds to banknotes, and then killed him and threw him into the Thames, all before his meeting with the other directors?"

Silver smiled. "Not quite. His plan was a good deal more involved than that—but perhaps I should let Mr. Barham explain it. Starting with how he tumbled to the whole scheme, possibly?"

Owen Barham nodded. "It was looking over the top floor of the firm for myself, and sitting in the seat that Miss Patience had occupied, that helped me surmise what had really happened on that Saturday morning. Miss Frumm referred to it as a 'magician's cabinet' at one point, and that was exactly what it was. Everything had been arranged to produce an effect, and make sure that the sole eyewitness saw exactly what she was meant to see."

Gertie Frumm dug her elbow triumphantly into her brother's rib, making him squirm in his seat.

"It was all precisely arranged. To do her typing Miss Patience had been placed, not at the auxiliary desk in Mr. Fairhope's office, which would have been the most sensible location, but at a desk in the outer room which gave her a clear view of both the office door and the corridor leading to the rear of the building, so that she could later swear that no one had exited in either direction. And who had instructed her to take that seat in the outer room? Who, in fact, had asked her to do the typing for Mr. Valdonato that morning?

"The more I considered the situation, the more my suspicions grew in one direction. The police, and everyone else, were so busy trying to figure out how Valdonato disappeared that they never asked themselves why. Why stage the disappearance in that way? If Immanuel Valdonato had wanted to vanish from his current life and begin a new one somewhere else, he could have removed the bonds from his safe at any time he pleased and simply walked away into thin air. No, the purpose of what occurred that morning could only have been to draw attention to the disappearance and the missing bonds–and who would have benefited from that except his murderer?"

Miss Patience threw up her hands. "Wait. Before you go any further, would you please explain how Mr. Valdonato disappeared from his office? There was no other way out, there were no secret passages or hidden doors…"

"Yes," echoed Jimmy Clough, leaning forward intently, "how was the trick done? Tell us, boyo."

"The simple fact is," Barham said, "that Immanuel Valdonato never left his office–at least, not alive. He was strangled with a piece of rope brought for the purpose shortly before eleven o'clock, most likely by Fairhope himself, and the body thrust into the kneehole beneath his desk. That's when the piece of watch chain that was discovered by the police broke off. Fairhope then stepped out, returned a few minutes later, and announced to you that Mr. Valdonato had vanished. Then, when you went for the police–that was one of the things that struck me as suspicious, that he sent you, instead of going himself–they transferred the body. He changed into a painter's suit like the one his confederate was wearing, they wrapped the body in a sheet, lashed it to a ladder, and carried it down the back stairs to a waiting lorry. By the time you returned with the constable Mr. Fairhope had changed back again and was ready to show the investigators the empty offices."

"Fairhope's scheme," added Silver, "was this: to make it appear that Valdonato had taken the firm's money and departed for points unknown. If it hadn't been for the unforeseeable circumstance of the body making its way to the surface of the river, the authorities would still be looking for a living Immanuel Valdonato, and Fairhope and his accomplice would have gotten away with their crime."

"And why was it he resorted to all that folderol?" asked Clough. "Couldn't he've taken the bonds in a much simpler way, if that's what he was after?"

Silver shook his head. "The bonds were registered in Valdonato's name, so that only he could have cashed them. In addition, he and Fairhope were the only ones who knew the combination to the safe where they were kept, so if they'd simply been stolen, suspicion would immediately have landed on Neil Fairhope.

"They might have forever stayed out of Fairhope's reach, in fact, except for his chancing to notice one day, in a pub near his home, a local laborer with a general resemblance to Immanuel Valdonato. He struck up an acquaintance with the man, one Abel Denley, and before long convinced him to become his partner in a scheme of murder and theft. You noticed the resemblance yourself, Miss Patience, on the day of the 'disappearance,' when Denley was playing the part of the painter, though you were too distracted to think much of it.

"It was Denley who played the part of their victim that following Monday at his bank, as well. That was why 'Valdonato' had developed a cold that prevented him from speaking and kept him well-muffled, and why his handwriting was so poor. Fairhope was sensible, too, in not immediately spending large amounts of the stolen money, and in not passing his accomplice his full share of the loot all at once.

"We must give the police some credit, though. They suspected Fairhope might have had a hand in the disappearance, but since Immanuel Valdonato was apparently alive and well at ten o'clock that Monday morning, and Fairhope was in a meeting with the other directors by eleven, there seemed no way he could have had time to murder him—especially since, as I mentioned, his valet claimed that Fairhope had returned to his villa before the meeting. Not to mention the improbability of anyone dumping a body in the Thames in broad daylight without being seen by multiple witnesses."

Clough shook his head with a knowing grimace. " 'Tis a bally shame, the love of Mammon."

"It wasn't greed alone behind it," Silver replied. "Fairhope is an inveterate risk-taker, which may be an advantage to a financier, I don't know, but it's resulted in heavy losses at the racetracks and clubs. The theft of the bonds was at least partially an attempt to ease that debt." He puffed cheerily on his pipe and reached for another scone. "Let that be a lesson to you, children, to steer clear of games of chance. You see what desperate measures such things can lead to."

# The Wainwright Will

The little Morris Cowley hummed north along the flat grey roadway, edging its bull nose through the stream of Saturday-morning sightseers and holiday-makers. Properly speaking it was a two-seater, but there were three of them squeezed into its belly, and it was Owen Barham, in the middle, who suffered the most from the arrangement: every time a shifting of gears was necessitated he gained another elbow in the ribs or knock on the kneecap.

The driver was a fellow student of his from University College, one Gerald or "Jerry" Carlisle, and the third passenger Carlisle's fiancée, Elspeth Greene. Despite the bright sunshine and blue skies the spring air was biting, and the three of them, especially in an open-topped vehicle, were bundled up against it: Carlisle with his driving cap pulled down over his wavy chestnut hair and an ulster wrapped around his athletic frame, Barham almost disappearing into his hat and overcoat, and Miss Greene with her cloche snugged down over her shingled blond hair and her fur collar turned up around her neck.

Earlier in the week the lovers had paid a visit to Barham's lodgings in Torrington Square to request his aid. The two young men were not close friends, moving in different circles as they did and pursuing different fields of study, but Barham's reputation had been steadily growing among his peers with each mystery he found himself involved with, and they had a puzzle of their own to be solved.

"My great-uncle, Wilfred Wainwright, passed away recently," Miss Greene explained, tapping her slim knees nervously. "He was a dear, sweet man, the postmaster in a little village north of here for more than forty years, but what you must understand about him was that he was simply mad about nursery rhymes. They were more than a hobby with him, they were his whole existence. When we were small, of course, my cousins and I, a visit to Uncle Wilfred's was an absolute delight, like travelling to Wonderland or some such place. He called us his 'Fiddlers Three,' and always had sweets and wonderful games for us to play. He had an imagination as vivid as any child's, you see. But as we grew older, I'm afraid, such things naturally faded away for us. Poor Uncle Wilfred…

"When he passed, he left a will behind, with specific and somewhat odd instructions–but instructions that sound every bit like Uncle Wilfred, I must admit. Aside from modest bequests to Mrs. Bramble, the village woman who cooked and cleaned for him–he never married–and to his surviving siblings, the bulk of his estate, along with his cottage and some other property, is to be distributed in one of two ways."

She took from her pocket a folded paper, a copy of the relevant part of the will.

"These are his specific instructions. 'To my dear young ones, my nephew Walter Ashbarry, niece Miriam Ashbarry, and niece Elspeth Greene, I leave the aforementioned monies and property, on one condition. Hidden somewhere on my little estate, in a place close to my heart and I hope theirs as well, is a token that will match one being held in the offices of Pulkinghorn and Bragg. When the token is presented to Mr. Pulkinghorn or the agent whom his firm appoints, the inheritance will then be granted to its bearer or bearers, as the case may be. I hope that they will still remember Little Robin Redbreast, the King of Spain's Daughter, Robin Hood, and the other dear characters of those happy days.

" 'If, however, the token has not been presented thirty days after the reading of this will, thus demonstrating that my little children have indeed forgotten me and the many delightful hours we spent together, I direct that the cottage and remaining tangible property be sold, and the resulting funds be used for the establishment of a Society for the Preservation of Mother Goose, to keep these treasures alive for future generations.' "

"Poor Uncle Wilfred," she repeated. "I'm sure we did neglect him these last few years, but you know how it is. One gets so busy with the trials and troubles of everyday life... And it isn't as though the legacy is a very great amount, but the money certainly would be beneficial. Father died just before the War, and the investments he left behind haven't done so very well, so that Mother could use the extra income. Not to mention that Jerry and I are hoping to be married soon, and we could use a little something to get started on."

"Have either of your cousins contacted you about the token your great-uncle mentioned?" asked Owen Barham.

"No, not for help or suggestions in finding it–not that I have any suggestions to give–nor even to say it's been found. I suspect they haven't had any luck so far. But Jerry's sure that with your assistance, we'll have a much better chance of finding the token. What do you say? Will you help us?"

After two hours of driving, with the anthill activity of London well behind them, they turned to the right onto a smaller road, and after several twists and turns came to a modest sign welcoming them to the village of Leverewich.

The first house they saw once they were beyond it was a half-timbered cottage with a heavy thatched roof and a sturdy front door painted red, surrounded by a hedge which had seen better days.

"This is it," Miss Greene announced. "Pull up, Jerry."

Carlisle cut the motor and dashed round to assist his fiancée from the vehicle, leaving Barham to extricate himself clumsily. The property on which the cottage stood was triangular in shape, formed by the angle of the high street and a smaller lane running behind the village. Up close they could see that the hedge was not simply untended, but someone had in fact pulled it open in several areas, breaking branches off in the process. The ground around the cottage too was disturbed, with fresh holes gaping here and there.

"My cousins have been here, clearly," Miss Greene said, surveying their handiwork with disapproval, her fists on her hips.

She stepped to the front door and withdrew a key from her pocketbook. "The lawyer, Mr. Pulkinghorn, was kind enough to provide me with a key, so I imagine my cousins were able to procure one as well." She swung open the thick oaken door, took one step inside, and stopped dead. Her hands flew to her mouth. "Oh!"

The interior of the cottage looked as though a great windstorm had blasted through it. The chairs were disturbed and rent in multiple places, while the drawers of the desk and the doors of the cupboards yawned widely. Rugs were scattered about and crumpled, revealing floorboards that had been pried loose in several spots, while the wallpaper hung from the walls in ragged ribbons. Paintings and prints had been pulled down and pried from their frames. All of the books had been removed from the bookshelves and strewn on the floor, but not before having their endpapers peeled apart. The figurines of nursery characters that lined the mantelpiece and the tops of other furniture were all upset, the ones with felt bottoms suffering only minor injury, while the rest had been smashed open. Even some of the bricks of the fireplace had been worked loose.

"Oh, how could they do this?" cried Miss Greene, close to tears. "I want to find the token as badly as they do, but this–this–"

"Brace up, darling," Carlisle said, giving her arm an affectionate squeeze. "We'll get our revenge on those cousins of yours by finding that token first, hm? So, where do we begin?"

He glanced at Owen Barham for suggestions, but the blond young man merely shrugged and blinked behind his eyeglasses. "We can only examine everything we come to," he said, "and perhaps find something they overlooked."

Carlisle, climbing over the wreckage, pulled open the curtains on all the windows to flood the space with as much light as possible. They were making tentative stabs at possible hiding places when the front door creaked open behind them and a booming voice filled the little cottage.

"What's going on 'ere? Great Lord A'mighty!"

The trio turned to find the village constable in the doorway, his blue uniform encasing a broad frame and heavy stomach. His eyes, surveying the shambles before him, were wide as saucers.

" 'Oo are you folks, now? And what's the meaning of all this? I'll be glad of a bit of explanation, if you please."

Carlisle, feeling he should clear the matter up quickly, cleared his throat and gave the constable a concise explanation of their presence in the cottage. As he finished his story the man regarded Miss Greene with a look of dawning recognition.

"You're little Elsie, then? I remember you, my girl. The other two as well, your cousins. Walt and Mirrie, isn't it? Though I don't s'pose you remember me. 'Enry Mott. Been the constable in Leverewich since before you was thought of, I expect." He shook his large head sadly. "And you say them other two did all this damage? There was some lights seen this end of the village a few nights back, close on to midnight, but by the time I was out of bed and 'ere with my lantern there wasn't a soul around, and the front door was locked up tight. Never dreamed they'd do a thing like this."

Miss Greene looked at him appealingly. "Will you help us search, Constable? You knew my great-uncle. Perhaps you'd know of a hiding place he might have used."

"The will," added Barham, "called it 'a place close to my heart.' Possibly you might have a suggestion as to what it could be?"

Constable Mott removed his helmet and scratched at his reddish-brown hair. "What was closest to Mr. Wainwright's 'eart was these nursery-rhyme characters of 'is—apart from you youngsters, I mean. Don't know 'ow much 'elp that is, but I'm willing to lend you a 'and in searching."

"Bless you!" said Miss Greene warmly.

After an hour, with the sunlight pouring in, the young people had removed their hats and coats and piled them on one of the armchairs. After two hours they were dusty, a little disheveled, and a shade dispirited. The four searchers had peered into and prodded every possible location they could think of, and found nothing even remotely resembling the "token" mentioned in Wilfred Wainwright's will.

Jerry Carlisle, frustrated and with a streak of soot alongside his nose, turned to his university comrade. "Well, Barham? Any sudden bright ideas? It seems as if all we're doing is following in someone else's steps, and to no purpose."

Barham, for his part, asked Constable Mott, "Did Mr. Wainwright ever talk to you about any particular nursery-rhyme characters? Ever mention any that he was especially fond of?"

The constable shook his head. "Not that I can recollect. Well, I've got to get back to my rounds, but it was grand meeting you all. Again, in one case," he added, beaming at Miss Greene. "I'll keep my fingers crossed for you and your 'unting."

When he had departed Carlisle said, "We might as well go on and search the upstairs. We're not having any success down here. Coming, dearest?"

The two of them climbed up to the rooms tucked beneath the stout roof, while Owen Barham began poring over the books scattered across the floor of the parlour. There was less to search in the two second-floor rooms, both because there were fewer pieces of furniture and because the late Mr. Wainwright's clothes and other personal effects had already been bundled up and sent off to the local aid society.

As they came down the stairs again, empty-handed, Carlisle muttered, "Can't see where else there is to look.

We've tapped on all the walls, trod on all the floorboards, poked our fingers into every drawer and cubbyhole we could find... Maybe this token of yours isn't in the house at all. Could it be hidden somewhere outside?"

"Let's go outside in any case," Miss Greene responded. "I could stand some fresh air."

They wandered out the back door, past an unheeding Barham, and stood looking over the property, breathing in the crisp country breeze. To their right, in the narrow end of the triangle, was a small garden and a birdbath, though its basin had been overturned onto the ground and the small plantlets were bent this way and that. To the left, the larger corner of the little estate was taken up by a stand of trees, their branches covered with bright green buds.

Miss Greene drifted over to the little patch of woods, followed by her fiancé. The first tree they came to was a chestnut whose trunk split off, roughly at stomach height, into multiple limbs. In the cleft thus formed a small wooden seat had been constructed, with its back carved with curlicues and painted, though it had chipped and faded over the years, and the slats making up the bottom had been pulled up out of position.

"This was the throne that Uncle Wilfred built for us," she said wistfully. "He made it with arms to begin with, but we quickly grew enough that we couldn't squeeze into it, and he had to take them off. It was one of the games we'd play–one of us would be prince or princess for the afternoon, and have to think up royal commands for the others, like performing dances or silly tasks." She sighed. "A lovely childhood dream, and all gone away now."

Carlisle was opening his mouth to say something soothing when Owen Barham emerged from the cottage, clutching an armful of books.

"It seems to me," he said when he reached them, "that the wording of your great-uncle's will must be a clue as to where he hid the token. Most people, when called upon to name storybook characters, will pick out Jack and Jill, Little Bo Peep, Humpty Dumpty, and so on–the most familiar ones. But Mr. Wainwright named three others, one of whom isn't even normally thought of as a nursery-rhyme character. Let's take them one by one, Miss Greene, and see if they have any significance for you. First of all, Little Robin Redbreast. Now there are several versions of his rhyme–"

The young woman giggled. "Yes, and one of them a rather rude one. I can still remember Mother's expression after hearing us recite that one! She couldn't stay upset with Uncle Wilfred for long, though; no one ever could."

Barham nodded. "That's the oldest version. In it the robin sits on a pole, but in others he's said to sit on a rail, a tree, or a wall. Do any of those things sound familiar from your childhood?"

"I'm not sure if this is anything," she said after a moment's thought, "but there is a nest box there, in the far corner of the garden, and it's mounted on a pole. If a robin happened to land atop it he could be said to be sitting on a pole, I suppose…"

Carlisle trotted over to the northwest corner of the property, where his fiancée was pointing, and stood on his tiptoes to examine the box. A corner of the roof had been pried up, making it easier for him to see inside. He returned shaking his head.

"There's nothing in it except some left-over bits of nest," he said. "Any other thoughts, old man?"

"Let's put the nest box aside for now," Barham replied, shuffling the volumes in his arms, "and move on to the next reference. That's the King of Spain's Daughter. The poem mentioning her runs like this:

> *"I had a little nut tree,*
> *Nothing would it bear*
> *But a silver nutmeg*
> *And a golden pear;*
> *The King of Spain's daughter*
> *Came to visit me,*
> *And all for the sake*
> *Of my little nut tree."*

"That's this tree behind us!" Miss Greene exclaimed– "the very one I was telling Jerry about, where Uncle Wilfred built a little throne for us children. But there's nothing to be found here. You can see where my cousins have pulled up the seat–there's nothing hidden under it, and the boards making up the back are too thin to conceal a hiding place."

"We have two possible points of reference, at least," Barham said, and turned to Carlisle. "Would you see if you can find a shovel? And perhaps a hammer, as well?"

Carlisle returned before too long, having located both items in a rear hall closet, and Barham set him to digging in a straight line from the chestnut tree to the pole holding the nest box. It was strenuous work, and Carlisle had a sheen of sweat on his forehead by the time he was finished–and all for naught.

"There's nothing buried anywhere along this line," he called to the others, leaning on the handle of the shovel with a disgusted sigh.

"Never mind!" Barham responded, and waved at him to come back. "It was a shot in the dark. It seems we have to take all three clues into account after all, as I expected. There's only one poem mentioning Robin Hood in these books…"

He fumbled through the volumes in his arms again, handing the hammer, which he had been holding in the meantime, back to Carlisle, and read out the nursery rhyme once he found it:

> *"Robin Hood, Robin Hood*
> *Is in the mickle wood.*
> *Little John, Little John*
> *He to the town is gone.*
> *Robin Hood, Robin Hood*
> *Is telling his beads.*
> *All in the green wood*
> *Among the green weeds.*
> *Little John, Little John*
> *If he comes no more*
> *Robin Hood, Robin Hood*
> *He will fret sore.*

"Can you recall, Miss Greene, anything to do with Robin Hood from your childhood?"

She shook her head. "This stand of trees behind us was a forest in our imaginations, and we did occasionally play at Robin Hood and his Merry Men, but that's all."

Barham nodded. "I think we can safely ignore the last stanza, and probably the first as well. That leaves us with Robin Hood counting his rosary among the weeds. We have no weeds to speak of, that I can see, but there's plenty of greenery above our heads. I propose we place Miss Greene upon her throne–this is where the hammer comes in–and proceed from there."

Carlisle set to work repairing the little wooden seat, while Barham stacked the books neatly to one side of the tree, and when the throne was as close to its original condition as it could be made the two young men hoisted Miss Greene up onto it. She swung her slender legs back and forth and laughed.

"Not so comfortable as it used to be, I must say. What do I do now?"

"My suggestion would be to first turn yourself so that you're facing the nest box squarely," replied Barham. "If you were telling your beads like Robin Hood, your hands would be in your lap or near your waist, but I think in this case you ought to raise them up above your head, so that they're in among the 'green weeds.' Do you see or feel anything?"

"No, nothing... Wait, over here there's something..." She stretched and craned her neck to see the object that she had bumped her left fingertips against. "Why, it's a nail, and yes, there's a string of beads attached to it, leading upward... If I can just..."

She gave a final, solid tug, and the object at the end of the beads abruptly shot forth from the hole in the branch where it had been tucked. It was an envelope, curled into a cylinder and encased in wax paper to protect it from the elements. She unfurled it. On the front of the envelope were written the words *To be opened by Abel Pulkinghorn, Esq.*

"This is it! This is it! Quick now, get me down from here. We have a lawyer to see!"

Carlisle grasped his beloved by the waist and swung her down to the ground, and the two ran hand-in-hand for the cottage and their things, while Owen Barham gathered up the books and the hammer and the shovel awkwardly and straggled along after.

Some little while later, in a dark and dignified office in Holborn, the three watched as lawyer Pulkinghorn, with a junior clerk standing by as witness, examined the envelope to be sure it was thoroughly sealed and then slit it open with his ebony-bladed letter opener. From it he withdrew a bauble depicting Mary and her lamb. He gestured to the clerk, who extended a slim case toward him, and from this the lawyer brought forth a second object, identical to the first.

Pulkinghorn's distinguished face creased in a subdued smile. "Congratulations, Miss Greene. They are a match, and that means, under the directions of your great-uncle's will, that you are the sole inheritor. The greater part of the estate, totalling almost four thousand pounds, as well as his real property, including the cottage in Leverewich, are yours. Have you any plans for the money?"

The young woman shook her head happily and responded in a gush.

"Jerry and I will use part of it for our wedding," she said, "and setting ourselves up in our own home–would you mind so very much living in a cottage in the country, darling?–and some of it will go to help Mother, and I even think we should give a part of it to Walter and Miriam–

minus the cost of repairing all the damage they caused, of course!... You are definitely invited to the wedding, Mr. Pulkinghorn, and so are you, Mr. Owen Barham, although–" she added, glaring at their bespectacled companion with mock sternness– "you are simply going to have to get used to calling me Elsie!"

The two young men strolling briskly along a certain curving terrace in Belgravia in the bright morning sunshine presented a singular pairing. They were boon companions and fellow students at University College, of almost the same age and of similar socioeconomic backgrounds; but there all resemblances ended. Owen Barham was slim and scholarly, with pale blond hair brushed straight back from his forehead, light blue eyes hidden behind round spectacles, and soft but precise speech that let only a faint trace of his East End origins sound through. His friend Jimmy Clough, on the other hand, was blackly Irish in both manner and appearance, with a head of dark curly hair and flashing dark eyes. His movements were athletic and his gestures energetic, and when he spoke it was in accents as thick as those of his relatives back in Cork, though he had in fact lived in Camden Town since he was a babe. In short, they were a veritable model of those two key strains–the Saxon, logical and down-to-earth, and the Celt, imaginative and intense–that had settled the British Isles in times long past.

It was the third day of summer, 192-, and the proud pillars and white-stuccoed fronts of the grand houses shone in the gleaming light. Across the way the trees and shrubs thrust vividly green leaves into the air. Up ahead, about midway along the crescent, automobiles were halting in front of one of the homes to deposit passengers–long, sleek vehicles in shades of silver and grey, for the most part, though one at least was a humble black taxi.

It was to that very address that they were headed, with a letter of introduction tucked into Clough's pocket. The home was the residence of General Sir George Abberley, famed veteran of the campaigns at Paardeberg and Ladysmith, and once or twice a year he and his wife, who were noted art collectors, opened the rooms on their topmost floor to viewing by a select group of fellow enthusiasts. The tour of the little private museum would take approximately two to three hours, and would be concluded with a luncheon in the house's smaller dining room.

The string of circumstances that had led to the two young men being included in this season's group was serpentine. Originally one pair of invitations to the tour had been extended to the Honourable James Pendlepoole, Member for North Hendon, and his wife. An unexpected sanitation committee question had arisen, however, preventing him from attending, and Pendlepoole, not wishing to offend a national hero, had personally written to suggest that his son and daughter would be more than pleased to take their parents' places. Notwithstanding their father's assurances, the younger Pendlepooles fancied themselves Bright Young Things, and had absolutely no interest in works of art that actually resembled their subjects. When, therefore, a sudden injury prevented his participating in the annual cricket match against "Devil" Dinsmore and the St. Marks eleven, Jeremy Pendlepoole did not hesitate to proffer the general's art tour as an incentive for Jimmy Clough (who, in addition to taking Art History as his secondary, had a reputation around the school as a rather decent "leggie") to step in for him. This new development necessitated another letter to the Abberleys, which the senior Pendlepoole in his disgust left to his wife to handle.

The pair were met at the front door by the butler, a tall and dampening fellow with a thatch of grey hair and a lantern jaw, who skimmed over the letter presented to him and gave the faintest of nods. It was merely a copy of the one sent to the general, and he was evidently well aware of its contents.

"Of course," he murmured. "You gentlemen are expected. This way, please."

They were expertly divested of their hats in something close to legerdemain and led along a short, wide hall to a sitting room where a group of individuals was waiting. As they entered their host rose shakily to his feet from a wingback chair and cleared his throat to perform introductions. Sir George was bent and wizened, with a beaked nose and black currant-like eyes that were still keen despite his nine decades. The hair that covered his scalp, spreading down into great mutton-chops on the sides of his face, was white as purest wool, and he supported his spindly frame on a pair of canes, so that with his hunched back and his elbows sticking out behind him he resembled some sort of hoary grasshopper.

Apart from him the room held seven others. He introduced his wife first, as any gentleman would, a plump lady of faded beauty but unmistakable bearing named Honoria. Next there were Harcourt Wynter, the celebrated Shakespearean actor and art connoisseur, and his much younger and peroxided current wife, that darling of the silver screen, Grace Copeland-Wynter. They were followed by Professor David Thatchwood of the Hornsey School of Arts, gazing imperiously through his gold-chained pince-nez, and his wife Beatrice, whose brown hair, plaited around her ears, managed to give her the look of a Pre-Raphaelite naiad sliding firmly into middle age. Lastly there were Miss Julienne Randell, contributor to *The Burlington Magazine*, with her oft-caricatured monocle dangling from her lapel, and the Reverend Septimus Harbottle, a round-faced Anglican clergyman with a bald crown, clutching the Holy Writ to the bosom of his black cassock.

After the social formalities had been observed the general led the group back out into the hall and around the corner to a private lift. The butler, who had evidently been lingering just out of sight, came forward to operate the contrivance. "Women and children first, m'dear," Sir George said to his wife, with a wheezy chuckle at what was evidently an old joke between them.

With the silvery chiming of a bell the cage rose, and then returned shortly thereafter for the gentlemen. When the group was united once more on the top floor their host took them along to the end of the corridor, and the tour began.

The Abberleys' museum comprised three rooms, all of them united by a common theme: the couple were avid collectors of small works of art, no single piece being larger than folio size, and many of them being quite a bit less, able to fit easily in the palm of the hand. The first room contained examples of Georgian and Victorian silhouettes; scrimshaw done on walrus tusks and whales' teeth; boxwood miniatures from the late Renaissance period; tiny Fabergé furniture and diminutive city scenes in glazed ceramic from the Ming Dynasty. The second room was dedicated to the field of printmaking, including woodcuts from feudal Japan, etchings by Dürer and Rembrandt, and lithographs by Robinson-Elmer. One work in particular that Owen Barham and Jimmy Clough lingered over was the famous double aquatint, *Xenophon at Gordyene*, depicting the Greek general and historian pausing with his troops before plunging down into the wild country of the Kardouchoi. The artist had made one print with dark blue and one with vivid yellow, changing the atmosphere from gloom and despair to hope and courage despite not altering a single line of the original image.

The third room contained the most traditional works of art, oil paintings and watercolours and so forth, pieces by Renoir, Waterhouse, Vermeer, and many others. It was while the group was in that gallery, toward the end of the tour, that the bell of the lift sounded, and shortly afterward a dark, slender young man in a sombre suit entered and made his way to Sir George's side. After a brief conversation he nodded and passed through into the next room.

He returned with alacrity, and once more bent his mouth near the general's ear, this time speaking in more urgent tones. The guests had not paid attention to him for the most part, but his reappearance and obvious tension caught Jimmy Clough's eye, and he nudged his friend Barham with his elbow.

Sir George glanced up at the younger man, raising his tufted eyebrows, and made a faintly disbelieving noise. He then turned and stumped across to his wife, and giving her a terse explanation under his breath he went off with the other man into the next room.

The tour continued, and Lady Abberley, who was nearly as knowledgeable about art as her husband, entertained her guests and answered their questions adroitly. At least twenty or twenty-five minutes passed before the two men returned. Sir George looked positively choleric.

He lifted his canes and thumped them in unison on the floor, once and then a second time, the iron ferrules clanging against the bare wood. When he had the full attention of everyone in the room he harrumphed loudly.

"Ladies and gentlemen," he rasped, "a situation has arisen which has never before occurred in this house, and it puts me in a rather discountenancing position. One of the pieces of art from the Centre Room, the yellow *Xenophon* by von Woringen, has–ahem–disappeared. When I state that it was clearly in its place before today's viewing began, you may understand the awkwardness of my position. Mr. Barbott and I hoped that it had simply worked its way loose from its frame somehow and fallen beneath a table or into a corner, but despite our thorough searching it is nowhere to be found. That leads me to a rather unpleasant conclusion, and the necessity of a distasteful request that will either verify or, hopefully, utterly disprove, my suspicion."

The implication of the general's words was not lost on his audience, and before he could continue his guests began speaking.

Harcourt Wynter, with his actor's elocution, said ringingly, "If you are implying that one of us–"

Miss Randell removed her monocle from her left eye, blinked, and replaced it. "Indeed! Why, the very idea!"

Mrs. Thatchwood turned to her husband in some confusion, and asked in a near-whisper: "David, what are they saying? Has the *Xenophon* been taken somehow?"

Abberley waited until their voices had died down before continuing. "Under the circumstances, loath as I am to have to say this, the only course appears to be for each of you to submit to a search of your persons, to be certain none of you has taken possession, even accidentally, of the *Xenophon*. The print is small enough that it could conceivably fit into a pocket or pocketbook. Of course, my wife and myself would include ourselves–"

At that point Jimmy Clough stepped forward boldly. "Beggin' your pardon, sir," he said, "but before you consider takin' any further steps you might just be wantin' to give an ear to my friend here, Owen Barham. He's had a fair bit of experience in these matters. He's a veritable sleuth-hound, you can take my word for it."

The general regarded Barham appraisingly and asked, with a touch of disdain, "You're a detective, young man?"

"Not exactly," Barham responded honestly, "but I have had some experience, as he said, in assisting the police in various matters."

"The Lendrich case and the Valdonato case, to name two you may've heard of," added Clough irrepressibly.

"You have some suggestions, then?"

"Only a request, Sir George. Might we and your–Mr. Barbott, is it?–examine the room where the missing print was hanging ourselves? It might be wise to eliminate some other possibilities before we come to the unpleasant measure you referred to earlier."

"The suggestion has merit, Sir George," murmured Barbott to his employer, low enough that the rest of them could not hear him clearly. "I must confess, I am out of my depth here."

"Hmph," the general said after a moment. "Very well. We shall await your conclusions, gentlemen, before any other measures are taken. First, though, Mr. Barbott, you might bring some chairs. I fear Lady Abberley is growing tired from this prolonged standing about."

That was the general's indirect way of referring to his own infirmity. Though he managed to dodder about under his own steam, supported on his twin canes, his strength was hardly what it was in his younger days. Barbott went out through the far door and across the corridor, and returned shortly with a pair of tall-backed side chairs for Sir George and Lady Abberley.

He then led Barham and Clough into the next room, to the place where the missing *Xenophon* had been hanging, in a double frame with its indigo twin. Owen Barham stared at the blank space on the left side of the frame for a little while.

"Tell me, Mr. Barbott, how likely is it that the print could have slipped out of its frame on its own? I'm afraid I know very little about paintings and prints, and how they're mounted."

The other man nodded sharply. "You've put your finger on the crux of the matter. I put that suggestion to the general to ease the situation, but it's inconceivable that this is anything other than a theft. None of the works in this museum has been handled in months. Even so, for a thief to have broken in here is equally unbelievable. The only real answer, distasteful as it is to contemplate…"

"How difficult would it be for someone to remove a print from its frame? Would it be an involved process?"

"I should think," Barbott replied, "that, using a reasonably sharp penknife, it would be a matter of only a minute or two. And the print is not much larger than a large postcard, as you can see from the one remaining, so that it could be slipped into an inner pocket with ease. Oh, what a state of affairs!"

"Well," Barham said gently, "we will at least try to consider every other possibility before we come to that one. You'll forgive me if I tread over ground you and the general have already covered, I hope."

Matching those words, the three young men made a second search of the Centre Room, but found nothing. In addition to the works of art covering its four walls, each room contained a glass-topped display table in the centre for those works too fragile to risk accidental contact, and Barham examined this carefully as well. They then moved on to the South Room and repeated the process, and with the same lack of results.

"Could a thief have gained access to any of these rooms from outside?" Barham asked.

"See for yourself," answered Barbott, and reached for the nearest set of curtains. The windows in the museum were few and small, and the general, well aware of the deleterious effects of direct sunlight on works of art, kept them covered at all times by heavy curtains of scarlet damask. Barbott parted the curtains just enough for Barham to take in the iron bars covering the outside of the window, close enough together that there was barely room for a man to slide an arm between them, as well as the thick layer of dust on the window sill.

"These rooms are cleaned only once or twice a year," Barbott said, drawing the curtains again quickly, "usually the day before one of the general's tours, and I doubt the maids touch the windows. I couldn't begin to guess when one of them was last opened, and with the bars on them, such an action would be pointless anyway."

"Still," Barham said, "for thoroughness' sake…"

He went quickly through the two rooms, poking his head into each remaining set of curtains, and returned brushing cobwebs from his flaxen hair. It was quite evident that none of the windows had been opened recently. Even granting the unlikelihood of a burglar scaling the side of a grand residence in Belgravia in broad daylight, there was simply no way such an individual could have reached the *Xenophon*.

"How many entrances are there to this floor?" Barham asked next. "We came up in the lift, but I assume there must be stairs as well."

"There is a back stairwell, but it's hardly ever used. This floor was originally no more than a set of attic rooms, you see, and it's only within recent years that this side of it was converted to serve as the Abberleys' private museum. Across the hall is still a jumble of storerooms. The lift was installed around the same time, and the staircase, which I understand is steep and cramped, was quickly abandoned in its favour."

Nevertheless Barbott led them out into the corridor, and to the plain white door at its near end. The door was unlocked, and like the windows it had clearly not been touched in some time, for when he opened it its stiff hinges gave a sharp creak of protest.

Jimmy Clough whistled briefly, with raised eyebrows. "Sure it is the thief couldn't've come through there without alertin' the whole lot of us!"

"I presume the same is true as far as the lift is concerned," murmured Owen Barham, as they peered into the dim shaft of the staircase, which was festooned with great strands of cobweb. "Am I correct, Mr. Barbott, that a bell sounds each time the lift is used?"

The other man nodded as he closed the stair door. "Yes, that's the general's idea of a safety feature–or perhaps simply a way to keep the household staff apprised of his movements, I'm not sure."

"How many individuals know how to operate it?"

"Only the butler, Twygg, and myself."

"In any case, we heard no bell until you arrived on this floor toward the end of the tour. So now," Barham said in an apologetic tone, "having eliminated any outside plunderer, we come to you, Mr. Barbott. You were alone in the room where the *Xenophon* was hanging. Could you explain to us your position in the house, and the reason for your presence in the museum?"

Barbott's face went ashen and his voice rose abruptly. "Do you imagine that I stole the missing print? It was I who brought its absence to the general's attention! Why, if–if you suspect that I have it concealed somewhere on my person, if you think that I've been carrying it about with me all this time, then by all means I will bow to Sir George's suggestion, and insist that I be searched here and now!" He concluded by thrusting his arms up and outward in dramatic fashion.

"We may yet come to that," Barham replied gently, "but for now, would you merely answer my question?"

Barbott took a deep breath and brushed at his coat front to regain his composure. "Officially I am Sir George's secretary, but in actuality I have been acting as secretary for both he and Lady Abberley for more than a year. I handle all of their correspondence, including penning any letters they may dictate, and I manage their calendar, which, with their advanced ages, is primarily filled with social engagements at this point–though the general does still get asked occasionally to speak at military clubs and memorial dinners. The next event on their schedule is a women's historical society meeting in Richmond approximately a week from now, at which Lady Abberley will be a guest speaker. Twygg and I were running through the arrangements for the trip down, and knowing that the museum tour was nearly finished, I came up to ask the general's permission to remove from the South Room a certain piece which Lady Abberley will be taking with her, to ensure that it was packed away in good condition for the journey–a Staffordshire pew group, which you no doubt recall seeing. It was while I was on my way through the Centre Room that I noticed the empty space on the wall where the missing *Xenophon* should have been, and I immediately informed Sir George of the loss."

"I see. Thank you. Is the missing print particularly valuable?"

Barbott appeared genuinely surprised by the question. "Certainly there are rarer pieces in the collection, and of course the two prints would be worth the most as a set, but even by itself, I have no doubt the yellow *Xenophon* would fetch quite a pretty penny from an unscrupulous art dealer or collector."

"Has the general ever published a list of the items in his collection?"

"No, not as far as I am aware. An inventory is maintained, for insurance purposes among other things, but that list is private, and only available to the general, Twygg, and myself."

"Have any of today's guests been through the museum before?"

Barbott furrowed his brow in thought. "Professor Thatchwood has been, though not his wife. Miss Randell has been, and the Reverend Harbottle has. I believe that's all."

Barham nodded and sighed. "It seems, then, that we've exhausted all the possibilities other than the one the general articulated. We had better make our report to him, and proceed to that next, unpleasant step."

He started to head down the corridor, but the secretary caught at his sleeve. "Then you–you don't believe that I took the *Xenophon*?"

Owen Barham smiled faintly. "You have the run of the house, Mr. Barbott. You could have removed the print at any time you wished and made it look as though a thief had broken in and carried it off. At the moment I can't conceive of any possible reason you might have had to take it this morning, while the general's tour was in progress, and then immediately tell Sir George that it was missing, when it would have been much simpler to 'discover' its absence after his guests had departed. My opinion, however, is not going to prevent you–and us–from having to demonstrate our innocence to the general's satisfaction."

The three young men returned to the North Room, where Sir George and Lady Abberley sat stiffly in their straight-backed chairs like aged sovereigns presiding over a small and discontented court. Under other circumstances their guests would have concluded the tour wishing for more time to study the many masterpieces. Now, having been forced to remain, their appetite for art had quickly dissipated and been replaced by offended muttering. They had broken up into two groups, the famous actor and his wife to one side and the Thatchwoods and Miss Randell on another, while the black-clad priest did his best to pour oil on troubled waters.

Barham made his report to the general in but a few words, though even that little was rendered redundant by the fact that he had entered the room with nothing in his hands, and Sir George manoeuvred himself to his feet.

"We have come, ladies and gentlemen," he announced, "to the moment of truth. The missing print has not been mislaid, or removed from the museum by any other means, so it must be in the possession of someone in this room. One by one, each of us will step across the corridor and submit to an examination of his person. I, of course, will volunteer to be the first."

Barham stepped close and spoke into the general's ear, and Sir George nodded.

"Ahem. Yes. Ladies, if you'll be so kind as to empty your handbags onto the table here before we begin, and then leave them behind while the search is proceeding."

The guests complied, with the expected amount of outraged muttering. One by one the women emptied their pocketbooks, from Mrs. Copeland-Wynter's tiny sparkling bag to Miss Randell's formidable sheepskin one, without revealing the *Xenophon*. It next fell to the secretary, Eustace Barbott, to conduct searches of the men in one of the dusty storerooms on the opposite side of the corridor, until at last it was his turn to be searched, by the Reverend Harbottle.

While they were awaiting the outcome of this procedure, Owen Barham strolled idly over to the centre display table, on which the priest had deposited the copy of Scripture that he had brought with him on the tour. It was a substantial volume, bound in glossy black leather and marked with scarlet ribbons, and the young man flipped through the first few pages, noting the elegant Gothic print and the intricate initials.

When Barbott and the reverend re-entered the room, the cleric held up his empty hands in a mute gesture, and it was the ladies' turn to submit to the indignity of being searched. Lady Abberley, despite her obvious discomfiture, carried out that task with thoroughness, but when the last of the ladies returned to the North Room, the result was the same.

The missing *Xenophon*, after all the searching that had been done, was nowhere to be found.

"Now where can the thing be?" Jimmy Clough whispered to his friend. "It wasn't taken by a burglar, it didn't fall into a corner, 'tisn't on any of these fine folk. It surely didn't evaporate into thin air... Haven't you any last ideas?"

Barham, looking thoughtful, did not reply.

Sir George glared in their direction and faced his guests squarely, with a rosy flush beneath his leathery cheeks. "Harrumph. There is... Ladies and gentlemen, there seems to be nothing left for me to say except to extend my deepest apologies to all of you. Whatever has happened to the missing *Xenophon*, I was clearly mistaken in imagining any of you could have had a hand in its disappearance. You are all, of course, still welcome to join my wife and myself at luncheon, though I most certainly will understand if, after this most disagreeable experience, you choose not to remain in my home a moment longer. Mr. Barbott will take you downstairs now."

The guests began to head out into the corridor, with the ladies at the front of the group, but Owen Barham cleared his throat and spoke up.

"Ladies and gentlemen—if you'll excuse me, Sir George—would you please make certain that you have all of your belongings before you depart? That nothing is missing?"

The men plunged their hands into their pockets with a variety of sighs, while the three women, who had emptied and refilled their handbags in full view of everyone, had no need to check. The Reverend Harbottle, at the rear of the group, gave a little laugh.

"In all the commotion," he said, "I very nearly forgot…"

He turned and strode back to the centre display table, stretching his arm out for his Bible, but Owen Barham reached the table at the same moment and placed his hand flat on its cover.

"Don't you think, Reverend, that a scriptural text might be appropriate at a time like this? Some balm in our time of confusion?" He lifted the heavy volume before the priest, his round face suddenly pale, had a chance to respond. "Allow me."

Before the eyes of all of them, Barham grasped the book by its front and back covers and holding it upside down, gave it a vigorous shake. After a second, equally firm shake, a medium-sized square of paper slipped free and dropped to the tabletop in all its xanthic glory.

"The *Xenophon*!" roared Sir George. "You had it all along! You—a man of the cloth! I ought to have you horsewhipped! I ought to have you tarred and feathered! I–"

His wife clutched his arm, and he subsided into a more normal tone. "Mr. Barbott, will you escort this–this black-robed bandit from my house forthwith, and deposit him on the kerb with all due dispatch? Let him find his own way back to his parish. You may rest assured, sir, I will be submitting a letter to Bishop Winnington detailing your abominable conduct! Get him out of my sight, Mr. Barbott, at once! At once!"

Harbottle snatched the Bible from Owen Barham's hands and scuttled out, his cassock flapping about his ankles, propelled firmly by the secretary's hand on his elbow, while the other guests stared after them in astonishment.

"Well, young man," Sir George said to Barham, "you managed to find the missing–stolen–artwork before it was removed from my house. Congratulations."

"I very nearly didn't," Barham replied mildly. "But all along, at the back of my mind, I had been wondering why a clergyman would bring a Bible along with him on a tour of a museum. Then, at the last moment, when every other possibility had been considered, I realised that the volume would make a very good hiding place for something flat like the missing print. Certainly, under ordinary circumstances, no one would have thought to look inside it."

"I cannot believe it," said Professor Thatchwood. "To think–a priest attempting to steal a famous piece of art. Whatever could have possessed him? Surely it couldn't have been for money, since the Church supplies all of his needs."

"All his legitimate needs," responded Miss Randell. "But who can tell what sort of vices men of that ilk might have?"

"Or perhaps he merely took it for the love of art," contributed Mrs. Thatchwood.

"At any rate," concluded Sir George, "after everything that has happened this morning, I could use another nip of sherry. You are all welcome to join me, so I suggest we move along to the lift, which should be returning momentarily. Women and children first, of course, women and children first!"

# The Yews of Yarborough

The summer sun shone gold-bright upon a landscape blanketed in hues of green, and glared so strongly through the train's windows that the two men soon reached for the blinds. When they had boarded at King's Cross Station for the journey north, they had been fortunate enough to find a compartment to themselves, and now the older of the two relaxed comfortably into his corner, puffing on the long clay pipe that was his trademark.

This was Thomas Beauclerk Silver, who was in his early thirties, with a somewhat narrow face capped by medium brown hair, and shrewd but kindly dark eyes. Taken altogether his appearance was such that he would not be particularly noticed in a crowd–which was a distinct advantage to one in his profession. He was a private enquiry agent by trade, and was travelling that morning on business.

His companion was a young man of perhaps twenty, with pale blond hair and light blue eyes closeted behind round spectacles. He was a student at University College, Owen Barham by name; the two had worked together in the search for the missing financier Immanuel Valdonato some months previous and had since become good friends. With the university shuttered for the mid-year holiday and Barham left with idle time on his hands, Silver had invited the lad to accompany him on his excursion.

"Not that there's anything really to investigate, I imagine," he said in explanation as the train rumbled along. "Apart from the man's age, the circumstances seem straightforward–and even that isn't unheard of in such cases.

"The deceased is one Major Reginald Munroe, who had recently returned to his hereditary demesne in Lincolnshire, in the village of Yarborough. He had roomed in London since the end of the War, and I spoke to his physician there–a fellow named Carsten Penbroke, one of those Harley Street specialists who make it a point to let you know just how valuable their time is. He unbent enough to spare me a few of his precious minutes yesterday, and the facts are simple enough. It's true that Major Munroe was only forty-four, but his family had an established history of heart problems. His father, for instance, died in 1916 of heart arrest. The major himself had something called ventricular arrythmia, which is a fancy way of saying that his heart didn't beat properly, and without proper care and medicine any day could have been his last. Penbroke had prescribed him quinidine, to be taken once daily at bedtime, and from his records Munroe had had enough to last him roughly a month–which is about exactly the time he was found dead. Munroe was not an ideal heart patient in any case: he was stubborn and prone to fits of temper and drank too much, and it was all Penbroke could do to impress upon him the seriousness of taking his prescription each day without fail. 'I tried to put the fear of God into him,' he said–'which is not easy to do with a man who refuses to admit the Deity's existence.'

"Major Munroe was found in his bed this past Wednesday morning, having passed sometime during the night. He had spent the previous day composing letters in regards to certain business interests, and seeing to other minor matters, including a stroll around the village where he lived. He had had no visitors, and received no parcels.

"My suspicion is that the departed found the combination of medicine and country air so palliative after the hustle and bustle of the metropolis that he decided he knew better than his doctor, and no longer needed bother taking the quinidine—with predictable results. However, as he had a life insurance policy through Arbuthnot's, those gentlemen desire a thorough review of the matter before it's declared closed and payment made. That is where I, and you, enter the picture."

"Who was his beneficiary?" asked Barham.

"Ah, that's always a useful question, isn't it? In this case the policy is to be paid to the deceased's wife, a Mrs. Violet Munroe—I might almost call her his ex-wife, except that the lady never actually sought a divorce from her husband, only a separation. She, in fact, lives in Yarborough as well, at the opposite end of the village from the major's manor house.

"Major Munroe was the last of his direct line. His nearest heir appears to be an uncle in Gloucester, one of his mother's brothers. His older brother, his only sibling, was killed at Bellewaarde in 1915, and his father died in 1916, as I said. His mother has just moved to the south of France, to the city of Toulon, to live comfortably on the monies her husband left her, and her change of address was what precipitated the major's own. The insurance policy dates from the major's marriage in 1916, and he apparently never felt the need to change the terms of it, despite his separation from his wife.

"I've arranged an interview with Munroe's servants, and afterward we'll talk with the local doctor, and the village chemist as well, if that proves necessary. I imagine that should give us all the facts we need."

That was all there was to tell of the case, and their conversation drifted on to other topics. At Lincoln they switched to a local which took them on to Louth, where they had to hire a car for the remainder of the trip, and arrived at last at their destination some minutes past noon.

Yarborough was a modest village, a collection of small brick cottages for the most part, grouped round the square tower of St. John the Baptist's Church and the dark bulk of the public house, with the chemist's shop at one end of the high street and the ancient residence of the Munroes at the other. To the west of the village rose the rolling series of hills known as the Wolds, while to the east, stretching out to the dark and lonely North Sea, were mile upon mile of bleak and monotonous marshland. The village drowsed in the heat of the day; there was the buzzing of insects and the chirruping of birds, and in the distance the sounds of workers in wheat and barley fields.

Silver drew the car up before the front doors of the manor house. The ancestral home of the Munroes was a high-fronted building of bluish-grey stone with the narrow windows and panelled doors of the Georgian period. The curtains were drawn in every window and there appeared no sign of life, but Silver was unconcerned.

"They'll be here, never fear," he said with a small smile, as he reached for the door knocker. "I telephoned from Louth station to make sure of it."

Owen Barham, who was perfectly well aware of that fact, only nodded absently.

The door was opened by a tall, angular man in his late fifties or early sixties. He was dressed in the expected cutaway coat and striped trousers, and the greyness of the house was reflected in the faded threads that ran through his dark hair. His face was long and bony, and his black eyes sat deeply in their sockets.

"Mr. Thomas Silver?" he asked.

"Indeed. This is my companion, Mr. Owen Barham."

The butler acknowledged the introduction with a brief nod and led them down the central hallway. The thick walls with their small windows held back the outside warmth, and the house was distinctly chilly. The ceilings were high, and the upper portions of the rooms were sheathed in a blue and purple Victorian wallpaper that managed to be both busy and dull.

They proceeded to the study, where a young woman in a dark grey uniform stood waiting, plucking nervously at her apron, and where the desk was already supplied with fresh notepaper, pens and ink. Silver smiled approvingly and waved the two servants to the pair of chairs that had been drawn up before the desk. He himself settled into the padded seat behind it as his young friend slipped unobtrusively onto a firmly-upholstered bench against one wall.

"Thank you for agreeing to meet with us, both of you," he began. "This is an unpleasant time, but I'm afraid these questions are necessary, and thankfully I haven't too many of them. To begin with, let me get your names down clearly. First, Mr. Armistead Dove?"

"Yes, sir." The butler sat stiffly upright in his chair, his knobby hands folded in his lap.

"How long have you worked for the Munroes?"

"My entire life, sir. My family have been stewards of this house for three generations, since my grandfather came on as a footman."

"And you, miss? Your name is Agnes Lumb?"

The young woman stared at him with her green eyes, vivid though set rather too closely together on each side of her long nose, and continued to twist her apron between her fingers. "Yes, sir, though most 'ereabouts calls me Aggie."

"How long have you been in the household?"

" 'Bout three years, sir."

"Are there any other servants, apart from yourselves?"

"The only other in the house recently has been the major's valet, a man named Wickes," Dove said. "We had another servant at one time, a lady's maid to Mrs. Munroe–the major's mother, that is–but she accompanied her mistress upon the move to the south of France a month ago. At any rate Wickes has been in London for the past week, attending to certain business matters for the major, and there's little he could tell."

"I see. Now, your master passed away this preceding Tuesday night, I understand, though he was not discovered until the next morning. Who found him?"

"I did, sir," Dove replied. "I brought him his breakfast in bed at the usual hour, eight o'clock. He did not respond to my knock upon the door, though that was hardly unusual, and as soon as I reached the bedside I saw the reason why. His body was contorted and the bedclothes were twisted this way and that, and his face, sir–well, it could not have been an easy passage. I sent Agnes for the doctor, but there was little hope of his being able to do anything."

"This was the village doctor, Dr. Edens, I assume?"

"Yes, sir."

"He examined Major Munroe and pronounced him dead at that time?"

"'Im and the vicar both, sir," added the girl. "They come to see the major together."

"Oh? I was of the impression that Major Munroe was not of a religious inclination."

"No, sir," answered Dove. "The major had pronounced opinions on the subject. He would not have been dragged into chapel at the point of a pistol."

"Is the doctor a religious man?" asked Owen Barham.

The two servants craned around to stare at the young man, who blinked back innocently, and returned their attention to Silver. The detective in turn regarded Dove patiently until the butler, taken aback, supplied the information.

"Not to speak of, no."

Silver glanced at his friend, but Barham added nothing to his original question, and the detective went on.

"To return to our original subject, then–did anything about Tuesday seem unusual or out of the ordinary? Did the major seem worried, or anxious, or vexed at all that day?"

"No, sir," Dove replied. "It was an ordinary day, far as the household was concerned."

"Had the major any visitors, or any messages, that day?"

"No, sir. He composed some letters, and carried them down to the post office himself in the afternoon, but that was all."

"Did he have any noteworthy visitors in the last month, any that perhaps stick in your memory?"

"No, sir…"

"There was Mr. Pennifeather, the vicar," put in Agnes doubtfully. "'E come to see the major a couple days after 'e moved 'ere from London, if that's what you're meaning."

"Was that at Major Munroe's request?" asked Owen Barham.

She turned and goggled at him, having seemingly forgotten that he was there. "Oh, no, the major weren't expecting 'im to visit. Vicar didn't stay long, either. 'Im and the major talked 'ere in the study for a few minutes, and then he left straightaway, and 'adn't been back since."

"I understand the major's wife lives at the other end of the village," Silver said. "Did he ever pay her a visit, or she him?"

"Not 'er," asserted Agnes. "First day the major arrived, 'e sent his man down to 'er house, to see if she'd be agreeable to 'aving 'im call on 'er, but she flat refused to see 'im. Sent Mr. Wickes off sharp like. The major left 'er alone after that."

"Out of curiosity, do you know what the trouble was between them, that caused their separation?"

"No, sir," Dove said firmly. "That was a personal matter, and none of our business."

Silver smiled faintly at that. "Now, as to the major's health, I've been told that he was prescribed a heart medication by his doctor in London. Was he in the habit of taking this medication regularly?"

"Each night, sir. His routine was to have a whiskey and soda before bed, sometimes more than one, and then he took one tablet from the bottle at his bedside, with a swallow of water."

"And had he taken his tablet the night before he died?"

"No, sir. Actually, as a matter of fact, the bottle he had been given by his doctor had been emptied a day or two before, and he had not been to the local doctor to get it replaced."

"Oh, but mind, Mr. Dove, the doctor'd sent 'im a new bottle," objected Agnes. "That Billy brought it round last week."

"Billy?" Silver asked.

Dove frowned at the maid. "You're mistaken, Agnes. You're thinking of another delivery altogether."

"But I saw it with my own eyes–"

"Never mind, Agnes," Dove said firmly. "Billy Ing," he explained, "is a local youth who works for the post office, delivering letters and packages. He makes deliveries for the other shops on occasion as well."

Silver nodded. "Would you happen to have the bottle from the major's doctor? It wouldn't be amiss for me to examine it while I'm here."

"I'm afraid it was discarded, sir. The major saw no need to keep it."

"Of course. One other question, again solely out of curiosity," Silver said with an apologetic smile. "What was the reason for the major's return to the village, and his family home? He didn't return here after the War ended, but took up residence in London."

"I can only make a guess," Dove said stiffly. "With the passing of the years Mrs. Munroe felt the need for a warmer climate. Her move to the French Riviera would have left the house empty. Her nearest relative, apart from her son, is a brother in Gloucester, and he would hardly be likely to take possession of the manor at his age. The major enjoyed the bachelor life in London, but I believe the thought of the family home sitting empty displeased him, and he may also have fancied the idea of playing the role of village squire."

"No doubt you're right. Now, if you don't mind waiting, I'll just write out a final version of what you've told me, and have both of you sign it…"

As the detective situated a fresh sheet of notepaper in front of him Owen Barham cleared his throat. "If it's all the same," he said, "while you're doing that I think I'd like to speak to the vicar."

"As you please," Silver said. "I can meet you at the vicarage after I'm finished here."

The young man left the house and walked back into the village. At the main intersection of the town, beneath an apple tree opposite the public house, sat a lad of about his age, clad in a faded blue coat a trifle large for him and munching on a fallen piece of fruit. He looked up from the upturned crate he was perched on and eyed the visitor curiously. Barham nodded to him in a friendly manner and continued up the lane that led to the churchyard.

He expected to find the vicar in the vicarage, as Silver had said. Instead he saw ahead of him two figures at the far side of the churchyard, one in black and one in drab brown: the cleric and his sexton, deep in discussion of the maintenance of the thick hedge that girded three sides of the property.

"Mr. Pennifeather?"

The vicar was a spare man of about sixty, with a white cap of hair and pale eyes, leaning upon a hand-carved walking stick. He swung about and peered down his aquiline nose at Barham.

"Ah, you must be one of our London visitors, come to learn about the late Major Munroe. Have you found out all that you needed?" Seeing the young man's expression, he added: "In a small place such as this one, I'm afraid, news spreads practically instantaneously. How can I help you, my son?"

"As you said, my friend and I are gathering some facts on the major for the insurance company. It all seems straightforward enough, apart from a point or two. I wondered if you might spare me a moment to discuss some details?"

"Ask."

"Is it true that you called on the major shortly after his return to the village? It was my impression that he was staunchly anti-religion."

"He was indeed. However, I had a question that I wished him to answer, and I was willing to beard the lion in his den to hear that answer."

"Was your visit successful, then?"

"I received the answer I expected. I was saddened by that, but not in the least surprised, though I had yet clung to some small hope that there could be another explanation. In point of fact, the major laughed soundly in my face."

The vicar rested his hands upon his walking stick and stared into the distance. In both profile and gaze he very much resembled a venerable eagle.

"It is not an easy thing to judge a man," he said, and then turned abruptly to what seemed another topic altogether.

"Do you see the hedge there, where our sexton, Mr. Gault, is cutting? And do you see that he wears thick gloves as he works? This hedge is woven together from yew trees that have been standing since I was a boy, and probably far longer; indeed, this entire village is ringed with yews. They have a great significance here, and a great significance to all Englishmen, if they but knew it. Yew wood is among the hardest of woods and yet flexible enough to have served for the famous longbows of Agincourt and Crecy. It has been used on the inside and outside of homes, for candlesticks and cabinets, for floors and walls and gates. Why, even this stick in my hands is of yew wood. Kings have required it, the Church has honoured it. And yet nearly every part of it is deadly poison, its leaves, its seeds, its oils. Animals large and small have been known to kill themselves by accidentally eating of it, and our Mr. Gault could easily join them if he were not careful.

"Every man, and woman, is the same. We are each of us given gifts and abilities, honourable and beneficent when used wisely, deadly as poison when used in the wrong way.

"The Munroe family, like the yew trees, have a long history here in Yarborough. They have been soldiers for the crown, fighting valiantly in places such as Balaclava and Kandahar. The major's brother fell in the attempt to hold the Germans back at 2nd Ypres. The major, for his part, made his mark on the far side of the world, on the Chinese coast.

"You're aware that the major was married, but that his wife and he were separated?"

Barham nodded. "We were told she lives at the opposite end of the village, and that she refused to see him when he returned."

"Violet Munroe," Pennifeather said quietly, "was born and raised in Yarborough. I've known her since she was a lass, and I learnt the whole story from her, shortly after her marriage.

"It began here in the village, before the great conflict ever broke out. Violet–Violet Enderby she was then–was at the centre of it. She was a fine, gentle girl, whose beauty was matched by her pious and sweet nature. It was inevitable that she should catch the eye of the eligible men in the neighbourhood as she reached her majority. There were two of them in particular vying for her hand: Amos Burrel, a strapping lad of about her age who worked as a hired hand at Sleight's farm, and Reginald Munroe, who was short and stout and a good deal older than her. He was not yet a major then, and already known for his temper and other failings, but he was also a Munroe, with all that that implied, and in her parents' eyes he was the better choice. Violet herself saw good in each of them, and consequently found it difficult to choose one over the other.

"Then the War erupted. Most of the men of these parts were sent to the Western Front, where Benedict Munroe was killed, but a small contingent was shipped to the Orient, to support a battalion of Welsh infantry. That was where Reginald Munroe was sent, a newly-minted officer, and as it happened, his rival for young Violet's hand was sent there as well, under his command. In a short time they found themselves fighting alongside the Japanese Navy, besieging the Germans in a place called Tsingtao. Munroe, who had a talent for languages, was appointed liaison between the two armies, and conferred often with the Japanese officers. The Germans had set up their defences on the hills that ringed the town, and they proved difficult to take. Both sides settled into a state of siege. After a month of fighting in disagreeable weather Munroe saw the opportunity he had been looking for. He persuaded the Japanese general that one hill in particular was the Germans' weak spot, and could be taken by a sustained frontal assault. Those men walked into a slaughter; the enemy rained down death from the heights with their Maxim guns, and if it hadn't been for the shelling from the ships lying off shore not a single soldier would have survived, English or Japanese. But in Munroe's eyes it had accomplished its purpose: his rival lay dead among the bodies that carpeted the valley.

"About a year and a half later his father died, and Munroe, who was a major by then, was granted leave in order to attend his funeral. While here in Yarborough he persuaded dear Violet to accept his proposal of marriage. It was all arranged in a rush, and he very much played upon her sympathies regarding his father's death and his brother's. I performed the service myself, in this very church, never suspecting the depths of which he was capable. Violet, poor child, learnt it quickly, his drinking and his temper and jealousy. On the night before he was due to return to his regiment, half-sotted and warning her not to look at another man while he was away, he poured out the whole awful story. The following day she came and related it to me, and then returned to her parents' house, and vowed never to see him again for the rest of her life.

"What sort of punishment would be appropriate for that kind of man? King David of old, when he had Uriah killed in battle, at least had the decency to withdraw the rest of his men from the enemy. Reginald Munroe was content to kill a hundred or more men, if it meant that Amos Burrel was struck down too. If twelve good men and true were to condemn him…"

"But it could never come to that, could it?" Barham asked quietly. "His crime happened halfway round the world, with the eyewitnesses men of another land. The War is over now, and any surviving witnesses have scattered to who knows where. How could he be brought to trial?"

"Just so. He said as much to me, when I confronted him with his wife's accusation. I needed to hear for myself what he would say. He had no qualms about admitting what he had done. It was only his wife's word against his by that point. He laughed and said that he had gotten well and truly away with his crime, and had not regretted his actions once. If the situation were duplicated, he said, he would not have hesitated to do the very same thing again.

"That, you see, was the sort of man Major Reginald Munroe was."

Owen Barham nodded, and bid the vicar farewell without asking the final question he had been pondering. He returned more slowly than he had gone, and his countenance was troubled. Though the sun pressed warmly down upon his back and shoulders, he was chilled, and the tranquil village lanes seemed disturbingly quiet to his urban ears.

As he reached the intersection of the high street he saw that Thomas Silver was standing in the shade of the apple tree, chatting with the young man in the oversized blue coat. Silver waved his pipe at Barham.

"I was about to start up the lane for the vicarage, but I saw you coming this way and decided to wait. Have you met Mr. Billy Ing? He was just telling me about the bottle he delivered to Major Munroe's house about a week ago for the chemist. I'm considering returning to the house and asking for a search of the premises, in case that bottle proves important."

"I imagine it's long gone by now. Tell me," Barham asked the young man, "was there a village meeting of sorts shortly after the major's return to Yarborough?"

"There was," Billy said, eying him narrowly. "In the public one evening."

"The vicar was there? And the doctor, and the chemist?"

"All three, aye. A good number of the men of the village were. I 'eard about it after, m'self, of course. They'd not invite me to a thing like that."

"And the Munroe steward, Armistead Dove?"

" 'E were."

"But not Major Munroe himself?"

"Well, 'e'd been away from the village for some years, so 'e wouldn't be expected to know the latest goings-on..."

Barham turned to his friend. "It's getting late, and I'm afraid I'm feeling famished. Could we stop for lunch before you question anyone else?"

"Certainly. There's the public house just here–"

"Actually, I saw a pleasant-looking tea shop outside the station in Louth when we arrived. It wouldn't be too much out of the way to drive back there, would it?"

Silver regarded his young companion thoughtfully and assented.

The establishment in question proved to be two streets from the Louth train station, a narrow building with a pastel front and waitresses in peaked caps. Between bites of cucumber and ham and cheese Barham related the story the vicar, Mr. Pennifeather, had told him.

"There were certain points I wondered about after you had questioned Mr. Dove," he said. "I wondered about the medicine bottles, of course, but I also wondered about the vicar's visits to the house. His first visit might have been simply in the exercise of his duty, to bring the major back into the fold, but the second, on the morning after his death–the only possibilities, apart from performing last rites, were that he had come to see something with his own eyes, to bring something to the house, or to take something away. And whatever the object of that second visit was, it was something known to the local doctor, or he would have not have called the vicar to come along.

"After my conversation with Mr. Pennifeather, I knew what the object of his first visit to the house was. That only left the second visit to account for. Clearly he had not come that morning to perform any spiritual services, since Major Munroe had remained decidedly atheistic up to the end. I could not conceive of anything he would have needed to see, especially at that particular time, and the servants said nothing about any objects appearing unexpectedly on the scene after the doctor's visit. On the other hand, we know of at least one object that should have been there and was not–a bottle of the major's heart tablets.

"I believe he came that morning to remove the bottle of tablets Billy Ing had delivered from the local chemist's, tablets which the deceased would have kept by his bedside, according to Mr. Dove."

Silver started to interject, but Barham held up his hand to forestall him.

"You have to understand, this is all purely conjecture, based on the things I've heard today. There is no proof, and I doubt you could find any at this juncture. It's my belief that the major recently had his prescription replenished, sending the request to the chemist via one of his servants, and the bottle that was sent round afterwards contained a lethal component. The local doctor was aware of this, and perhaps being frightened to remove the bottle from the scene himself, brought the vicar along when he was called to view the body."

"So you think the chemist…?"

"Not alone. I believe the vicar, after his conversation with Major Munroe, called a meeting of the responsible men of the village to decide his fate. That was what he meant by it being difficult to judge a man–not a reference to forming an opinion about someone, but a reference to passing sentence on him. The chemist was to make ready a bottle of tablets, one or more of which, I suspect, contained a preparation of yew. Yew poison is quick-acting and quite potent, and its effects would very much resemble a heart attack–and, in view of the history Mr. Pennifeather related to me, would have seemed both appropriate and convenient. After the poison had done its work the doctor was to pronounce the victim dead of natural causes, and the steward, Dove, was to swear there never had been a second bottle of tablets. The vicar would help dispose of the evidence."

"You're certain of all this? If you are, then I need to consult with the police."

Barham shrugged. "As I said, any evidence is long gone by now, and if they have a village policeman in the place, he's as likely to be in on their scheme as not. The official view of the case would no doubt be a skeptical one."

"But this is monstrous!" Silver objected, pitching his voice low so the other diners would not be alarmed. "We can't let the lot of them get away with murder! This is England, not some island of bandits, dispensing justice however they please. We have such things as courts and laws in this land."

Owen Barham took a long sip from his cup and replaced it in its saucer contemplatively. "Is it murder? Reginald Munroe was responsible for the death, not only of Amos Burrel, but of countless young men, the greater number of them likely from this very district. It's true there was no formal trial, but they had no need of one. Munroe freely confessed his guilt both to his wife and to the vicar. All that was left was for them to determine a suitable punishment, and the arrangement for carrying it out. In a sense it's the very embodiment of English justice: the major had acted grievously against his community, and his community pronounced judgement on him–and in an orderly manner, which is why Mr. Pennifeather spoke of twelve men condemning him.

"You know your business far better than I do, of course, but it appears that you have only two feasible courses of action open to you. You could return to Yarborough and attempt to convince the vicar to confess the villagers' actions to the outside authorities, or you could submit your report to Arbuthnot's as it is, and recommend that they consider the matter closed."

Silver turned his head and stared out the tea shop window, remaining deep in thought for quite some time, as the building quivered to the arrival and departure of the trains at the nearby station.

# The Zealot

# of Zachary

It was on a long, shimmering summer's afternoon that Thomas Silver and Owen Barham arrived in the village of Teignmouth, in the county of Devonshire. They had taken the Great Western Line from Paddington, and as the hectic crowds of the metropolis had dwindled away behind them they had passed through green forests and rolling meadows, across the fabled downs of Wessex, until at last they found themselves among the bleak moors and rocky hills that lowered over the River Teign.

Thomas Beauclerk Silver, narrow-faced and dark-eyed, was a private enquiry agent. His companion, on the other hand, was a pale and bespectacled student at University College in London, who had been of some assistance in one or two of his cases. The two were now good friends, and with the long holiday upon him the younger man was free to accompany Silver on yet another excursion.

The train station was near the centre of the village, and the two men were able to walk to their destination, the quayside. This was not the grand pier and the broad stretch of beach so beloved of holiday-goers, but was on the opposite side of the hook-shaped cape, on the inner harbour. They were met there, at the top of the Old Quay, by a trim man with a dour expression, his hands shoved into the pockets of a heavy worsted suit. This was Inspector Blackett, who had been sent out from Scotland Yard to look into the situation in the area, and he did not appear especially pleased to see them.

He shook their hands briefly and they walked slowly along the wharf, while the din of seabirds and the cries of workers filled the air. The two professionals, public and private, strolled side by side, and Owen Barham trailed after, his keen ears following their words despite his air of wide-eyed sightseeing.

"We'd better get down to brass tacks, eh?" began Blackett. "The sooner you hear the facts, the sooner you can direct attention to the ways I've fallen down on this case."

"Not at all, Inspector," Silver replied kindly. "As I explained to my young friend on the trip down, I'm not here to make trouble for you, or to try to take charge of your investigation. I've been hired by Pangborne & Sons, the firm that owns the ships in question, to provide you with any assistance you might require to get to the bottom of the matter. The longer the ships are delayed in port, the more their schedule is thrown off, and the greater the loss to the company, as I'm sure you appreciate."

"You needn't bother to soft-soap me, gentlemen," Blackett returned bitterly. "I haven't made an inch of progress in the time I've been here, I admit it. We have the blasted thing by both ends, but the middle remains out of our grasp entirely...

"Here are the facts. Eight months ago a gang of burglars began striking chateaux and country houses in the Loire Valley region of France. Shortly afterwards the stolen items, jewelry and silver and so forth, began appearing in London. They weren't entering the city by the usual route, by way of Calais and Dover, but from some other direction. The French *Sûreté* followed the smuggling route to the port of Brest, in Brittany, while we at Scotland Yard were able to trace our end of the trail back to Exeter. From there we were able to narrow the possibilities down. The dockyards at Plymouth have been under the management of the Royal Navy for some years, so there's very little commercial shipping being done there, while the shallowness of the estuary at Exmouth limits the number of freighters that put in to it. That leaves Teignmouth.

"At first glance it wouldn't seem this is the place, either. There is a dockyard here, but the majority of the men in the town work at sea, cod fishing off the Newfoundland Banks the greater part of the year. However, we were able to learn that a certain company, Pangborne & Sons, has a pair of ships that regularly travel between Brest and Teignmouth, the *Antioch* and the *Dora Rose*. They make the trip twice a week, sometimes three times, carrying bolts of cloth and barrels of all sizes, half of them empty and half of them loaded with dyestuffs.

"My sergeant and I were sent down here two weeks ago. For two weeks we've searched both ships each time they've reached this dock, from stem to stern, and their captains have seen our faces enough times to come to loath them. With the help of the local constable we've sounded out the walls and floors of each one–pardon me, the bulkheads and the decks–in hopes of finding hidden compartments. We've gone down into the holds and peered into the empty barrels with lanterns. We've run thin steel rods down into the casks holding dyes, as well as between the rows of cloth. We've peered over the sides to check for ropes being dangled below the waterline. My poor sergeant has shimmied up the masts to make certain nothing was being secreted up there in midair. We've trailed the crewmen once they were off the ships to see who they might come in contact with. And all of it for nothing. So far I've seen no hint of any secret hiding places or means by which the stolen goods could be moved–and yet they are. The items in question are continuing to reach Exeter, right under my very nose."

Blackett, in a gesture of frustration, pushed his bowler to the top of his forehead with his index finger. "I'm no sailor, but I hope to have some common sense. If the gang's loot is going aboard a ship at Brest, and there's no stopping point in between, then it must be coming off here at Teignmouth. There's no two ways about that. But how is it being done? Is one ship involved, or both? I would be more than delighted if you gentlemen can tell me what it is that I'm not seeing."

The inspector's ironic tone indicated that he had little confidence in their being able to do so. By then they had passed the grand hotel which sat directly at the water's edge and had reached the new quay. Blackett stopped in front of the first of two steam freighters, long dark vessels that rode relatively low in the water.

"I had them hold off on unloading the cargo on this latest trip until you were able to arrive, and kept the crew confined to the ships. They'd all like my head at this point, you can be sure. If you're ready, we can go aboard and begin the process of searching all over again."

As Thomas Silver turned his head toward the inspector, he saw that they had been joined by a fourth individual, the local constable, stolid and dignified with his dark uniform and drooping moustache.

Silver held up his hand in a questioning gesture. "During your other searches, was the crew free to move about, or kept in one place in the ship? Forgive me for delving into the obvious."

"No, I made certain they hadn't any opportunity of larking about behind my back. I had them gathered in the captain's cabin, under guard, this last time. I did that with both ships."

"And the stolen items couldn't have been concealed on their persons while you were searching the ships?"

"Not in the quantity in question–unless the entire crew of one of the ships is somehow involved, which I think is hardly likely."

Silver nodded, ruminating over everything they had been told, and Blackett asked, "Any further questions, gentlemen?"

"Have there been any other unusual incidents in the area?" returned Owen Barham, speaking up for the first time.

Blackett stared at him. "Any other–? Isn't one conundrum enough to grapple with?"

Silver, who was used to his young friend's abrupt turns of thought, said, "It's a fair point. If this gang began their operation here eight months ago, perhaps the locals noticed something or someone out of place around that time, or since, without realising the significance of it."

"You can be sure I haven't overlooked anything promising," Blackett replied. "We made inquiries when we first arrived, but turned up nothing meaningful. Teignmouth gets a good number of pleasure-seekers throughout the year, but there haven't been any visitors that particularly struck the townspeople's attention. The only thing out of the ordinary," the inspector added with what was almost a smirk, "is the local prophet–but that's at the next village over, at Zachary."

"Prophet?" Silver asked.

"About eight months ago the divine of some obscure sect showed himself in the main street in Zachary, the little hamlet on the opposite side of the harbour." Blackett pointed down the length of the quay, at the tip of the cape and the rolling water beyond. "He declared he was there to exorcise some imp or hobgoblin that's supposed to haunt the countryside behind the village. He took up residence in a cottage on the hilltop, to face the enemy on his own ground, and he's there still, as far as I know. It goes to show the sort of superstitious beliefs they have in these out-of-the-way places."

The constable too shook his head sorrowfully at the follies of "those people."

Barham, gazing thoughtfully into the distance, asked, "Is there anyone here who might know more about that, who might be able to provide me some details on the legend?"

"Constable Ball can tell you, I'm sure," Blackett replied impatiently.

"There's Professor Petherick," the uniformed officer said. " 'E's by way of being what they calls an 'antiquarian.' 'E's written a book on such things, and 'e sends articles in to the *Post* now and again. 'Is 'ouse is in Carlton Place, matter of fact, just a street or two over from 'ere."

"Do you mind," Barham asked Silver, "if I call on the professor while you begin your examination of these ships?"

Silver raised his eyebrows, but after all it was he who had been hired to investigate the smuggling ring and not young Barham, so he said only, "If you feel you must."

Barham made his way to Carlton Place, following the constable's directions, as the gangplank was lowered for the others to board the *Antioch*. The professor's home was not difficult to locate, a narrow building nestled between two larger businesses, with green-painted shutters and window boxes holding sprays of gladioli. The door was opened by a woman with a long face and iron-grey curls, whom he at first took to be the housekeeper, but proved to be the great man's sister.

"My brother is at work in his study at the moment," she said primly, "but I will see if he can be disturbed. Step inside, please."

Barham did not have to wait long. Professor Adam Petherick was long-legged and barrel-chested, with reddish-brown hair liberally threaded with grey and a curly beard straggling to twin points on his shirtfront. He rose from behind his desk, in a room thick with papers and volumes of all sorts, and shook his visitor's hand. Like experts of all stripes, he was quite willing to speak at length on his chosen subject, once Barham had explained the nature of his enquiry.

"Ah yes, the holy man of Zachary. His name appears to be Jasper Crang, and he's become something of a well-known figure there in the past months. He is often to be seen in the main street, exhorting his listeners to remember the Lord before it is too late, and to keep themselves at home of nights as good Christians should. I've never been able to learn exactly what church he represents, some non-denominational one I suspect."

"And it was eight months ago that he arrived in the village?"

"It was on St. Andrew's Day past, so… yes, eight months would seem to be correct."

"I understand he has taken up residence on a hilltop behind the village, to battle some sort of spectre?"

The professor smiled tolerantly. "Yes, he's our West Country version of Anthony of Egypt, taking arms against the infernal forces. In this case it's the Pixies of the Ness he has set himself to defeat–you may decide for yourself whether there is a band of pixies involved, or simply one pixie, the stories differ–and I've heard he intends to reside in a little cottage on the hill until his task is done. The tales of a spirit or spirits haunting the Ness are from long antiquity; the fairies and pixies of olden time were a more mischievous and malevolent bunch than the versions our Victorian fathers handed on to us…" Petherick rose once more, without warning. "If you don't mind walking with me, it might be easier to show you the spot than describe it to you. Florence, where is my hat?"

"In the same place as always, Adam dear," his sister called back from the other room. "On the coat-stand."

Their peregrination took them along the leisure side of the waterfront, past the celebrated public park known as the Den and the lighthouse, to the end of the promenade, where they stood looking out across the water to the opposite shore. Petherick pointed out the headland, standing dark green against sea and sky, with a cluster of dull houses at its base, huddled behind the breakwater.

"That is the hilltop known as the Ness," he said, "and the village of Zachary below it. The pixies are said to freely roam the dense woods that cover the Ness, and gather atop it for mysterious ceremonies. The evidence of this comes chiefly in the form of lights seen flickering among the trees, although there are one or two stories of men who were riding across the countryside to the village having their horses spooked or hag-ridden…"

"This is a very old legend, you said?"

"Yes, indeed, although oddly enough it seems to have had something of a revival lately. When I first gathered anecdotes of the Ness they came from the very oldest inhabitants of the village, some of them repeating stories they had heard from their elders. But in the last few months a fresh crop of accounts has arisen, along the same lines of course: ghostly lanterns moving through the woods and coloured lights dancing on the hilltop. Perhaps the fair folk have been stirred up by this Jasper Crang's presence on their sacred hill."

"His cottage is at the very top of it?"

"Yes, a little rude place in a clearing, the dwelling of some hermit of old. You probably can't make it out among the trees–it can be spotted more easily in the colder seasons, from the smoke rising off the chimney–but it can be seen clearly from the sea, I've been told."

"When are the spectral lights usually seen? Is there any particular time?"

"At night. Other than that, I have no particulars."

Owen Barham regarded the Ness for a time in silence, then asked, "How do the villagers travel from Zachary to Teignmouth? By means of the bridge I see there in the distance?"

"No, that's the railway bridge. Only a few foolhardy souls are tempted to cross by that means. The nearest bridge for regular use is some distance upriver, at Newton Abbott. One could always sail or row across from Zachary if needed, I suppose, but it's rare for anyone there to do so. It's Newton Abbott that they travel to in order to experience cosmopolitan life."

Barham thanked the professor for his time and returned to the wharf where the two steamships in question were docked. The search of the *Antioch* had just been concluded, and unsuccessfully, from the sour look upon Inspector Blackett's face as they stepped from the gangplank onto the quay.

"Did you learn anything of interest?" asked Thomas Silver of his young friend.

"I'm not certain," Barham said. "I have the beginnings of an idea. What about you?"

"We're completely at sea so far," Silver replied drily— "in a manner of speaking."

"Are we ready to start on the second ship, gentlemen?" Blackett asked heavily.

"I wonder," Barham mused, "if, instead of searching for something that shouldn't be there, we might do better to look for something that should be there, but isn't."

He added nothing more to that cryptic pronouncement, however, and Silver nodded to the inspector. The group climbed aboard the *Dora Rose*, and after a lengthy and minute examination of the entire vessel, found themselves as empty-handed as before. At the end of it they gathered in the captain's cabin, where the crew was sequestered.

"Captain Yeo," Blackett said, and the words seemed to stick in his throat, "I thank you and your crew again for your patience. Having found nothing out of the ordinary aboard, I am going to release your ship and crew to resume their normal activities. I have already told the captain of the *Antioch* the same thing."

Owen Barham cleared his own throat. "Before we depart, may I ask a few questions? You'll forgive me, I hope, Captain, if they're elementary or foolish. All this is quite new to me."

Those assembled stared in some surprise and curiosity at the young man. He blinked owlishly behind his spectacles at becoming the focus of attention.

"First of all, what is your usual routine on one of these voyages? Begin at the docks in Brest, if you would."

Yeo shifted his stubby pipe around his mouth and answered in an aggrieved tone. "Our shipping days start at sunup. The freight's been brought dockside the night before, and we begin loading it on board first thing. That takes most of the morning, then there's the checklist to be run through before we disembark. Any ship's captain who'd leave port without making sure his vessel is seaworthy, even if he's made the trip a hundred times before, is a fool. By the time we're halfway through the list it's noon, and everything stops for the lunch break. The Frenchies take their meals seriously, and there's no rushing 'em. Result is, we leave Brest between one and two o'clock. Takes us a little over six hours to make the trip to Teignmouth, which means we generally arrive here about eight in the evening. We take the rest of the night to unload our cargo, then the crew kips down for a few hours' rest, and then it's time to be up and readying the ship for the trip back. By noon of the next day we're sailing into Brest harbour again."

"Tell me about the tides here at Teighmouth. Do they ebb and flow at the same time each day?"

Yeo chuckled involuntarily at this lack of knowledge. "No, lad, the tides change regularly, year in and year out. That's why they print tide tables. The harbourmaster'll have them, if you've a need to see 'em. Not that the tide's much of a concern for us on the *Dora Rose*; with our engines we can ride out anything the sea throws at us."

Barham nodded. "Have you or your crew seen any unusual lights when sailing into the harbour here? Particularly in the direction of Zachary?"

A murmuring ran through the crew, and one of them spoke up: "You mean the lights on the Ness?"

Barham nodded.

"Ar, we've seen it, what looks to be flames a-flickerin' on the 'illtop, in different colours. Seen it more'n once."

"For many years?"

The man speaking scratched his head and ducked his chin. "Well, no, come to it, been just this last year or so we been a-seein' it for ourselves. Afore now it was only stories we'd 'eard, from our granfers and grandams, when we was wee nippers."

"Do you see these lights every time you enter the harbour?"

"Some nights we do, some we don't."

"Any other unusual lights or activity come to your notice?"

The mumbling among the crew resumed, and another sailor raised his voice hesitantly. " 'Ee wouldn't be meanin' the St. Elmo's lights, would 'ee, lad?"

Barham raised his eyebrows and waited patiently. Captain Yeo moved his pipe restlessly from one side of his mouth to the other, and Blackett muttered to Silver about the pointlessness of these questions.

The seaman continued in his halting fashion. "Every man's been to sea any length of time's seen they lights. They's a kind of vapour, a-flickerin' round the top of the mast and skippin' along the riggin', especially when a storm's a-comin' up. Why, just this past week, I even seen 'em dancin' the opposite direction, down the side of a ship to the water…"

"Where was this?"

"Here, comin' into Teignmouth 'arbour, not this last passage but the one afore it. I 'appened to be on deck, and I seen the lights a-crawlin' down the port side of the *Antioch*. She was sailin' ahead of us, as she usually does."

"Do you recall which direction the tide was running at the time?"

There was a general shaking of heads in response. Owen Barham had no further questions, and the investigators debarked the ship without delay.

That evening, as Inspector Blackett and his two visitors took a meal of beef pasties and watery mashed potato in a dockside inn called the "Bird-in-Hand," Barham endeavoured to explain his ideas about their situation.

"It struck me at once that the timing of the various events in this area–the activities of the smuggling ring, the arrival of the evangelist in Zachary, and the subsequent renascence of the lights on the Ness, all of them eight months ago–cannot be a coincidence. I believe the coloured lights on the hilltop, which could be easily achieved by adding cuprite or other minerals to ordinary flame, are a signal to the gang members at sea."

"And if they are?" retorted Blackett. "You've told us yourself that there's no way across the harbour from there. The nearest bridge is at Newton Abbott, which means the stolen items have to be travelling out of Teignmouth, and that brings us back to the original problem. How are they reaching the docks here? Every single search of those two ships has been fruitless."

"I imagine," Barham said mildly, "that you and I are the same, Inspector. As lifelong Londoners, used to brick and cobblestone, we tend to view the water as an obstacle to be overcome. But to the men of these shores, born and bred to it, the seas and rivers are simply another type of highway.

"It's my suspicion that the stolen items are being brought over on the steamship *Antioch,* but are not reaching the Teignmouth docks at all."

Blackett stared at him. "Not reaching the docks? The devil do you mean?"

Thomas Silver, who had an inkling of his young friend's meaning, started to respond, but Barham cut in ahead of him.

"I think," he said, smiling, "the best way to show what I mean would be to catch the culprits in the act. When do the steamers return to Teignmouth?"

"Two nights from now is the next scheduled trip."

"Then we'll be waiting. You'll want to call for boats and additional men, and cable to the harbourmaster in Brest beforehand, to make sure you have the information you need, and to delay the freighters' passage, to be certain they arrive here after nightfall..."

So it was that two nights later, a few minutes before ten o'clock, a small boat with four men in it floated on the waves some distance off the Ness. The craft, like the others holding closer to Zachary and Teignmouth, was equipped with a motor, now silent, as well as a set of muffled oars to help maintain its position. The men aboard–Silver, Owen Barham, Inspector Blackett, and his sergeant, a stout fellow by the name of Tulley–were dressed in dark clothes, with woolen caps pulled low over their eyes.

The sky was half-filled with thick clouds, and the moon shone but wanly. The air was sluggish. In the distance, barely noticeable at first over the rustling waves, came the rumbling of the two steamships belonging to Pangborne & Sons. Before long the lights of the ships could be seen, drawing nearer as the pilots aligned their prows with the entrance to Teign estuary.

Inspector Blackett looked back over his shoulder, at the coloured lights flickering in the clearing atop the Ness, and then turned his face forward doggedly.

When the ships drew close enough that their wakes increased the slap of water against the front of the little boat, the men inside hunched down, keeping their heads as low as possible and their hands out of sight. In such overcast conditions there was little chance of their presence being noted by any observers, but it was better not to risk the gleam of moonlight on bare skin.

The two steamships powered past. As the *Antioch*, in the lead as usual, drew ahead, there was movement along its port side, and a series of pale glints, faint crescents that waxed and waned in no particular pattern, slid down the side of the ship and spread out on the surface of the water. The men waited.

A dark shape emerged from the gloom. The glowing crescents lifted off the water and disappeared one at a time into what could only be another vessel. As the last crescent raised into the air Inspector Blackett lifted a whistle to his lips and sent several shrill blasts echoing across the waves. At the same time Sergeant Tulley and Silver flipped back a heavy cover in the bottom of the boat to reveal large lanterns which they hoisted aloft, sending forth blazing beams of light.

In the revealing rays was another little craft like their own, possessing both motor and oars, as well as two men resentfully shielding themselves from the glare with upraised arms. Nearer to shore there was dazzle and commotion, as other boat motors throbbed into life and other lanterns were lifted, while on the far side of Zachary still more men raced up the path that led to the top of the Ness…

"It was more or less as you described it," Inspector Blackett said to Owen Barham some time afterward, at the "Bird-in-Hand." "The man in the front of the boat was this so-called preacher, Jasper Crang. That's his real name, by the way, although we at the Yard know him better by other names, and he's the head of the gang. He was born not far from here, and has spent most of his life involved in such things as burglary, forgery, and confidence games.

"The stolen goods were inserted into small barrels at the factory before arriving at the docks in Brest, and these were marked with luminous paint. That was what we saw being dropped into the water. The purser on the *Antioch*, a man named Thrush, was the inside agent on board: he lowered the marked barrels over the side of the ship by rope just before it entered the harbour, and altered the manifest to reflect the reduced number of barrels remaining in the hold. We were able to prove that by comparing the records we got from the harbourmaster in Brest, as you suggested.

"Crang's idea of using the old legends about the Ness as cover was his most clever stroke. Smuggling has a long history in this part of the country, and similar things have been done before. His streetcorner pronouncements served both to explain any lights seen on the hill and to keep the villagers of Zachary from investigating too closely. In reality the fire on the hilltop, as you suspected, was a signal to Thrush: if the flames were varicolored, the tide was running out, and he was to lower the barrels on the port side, where they would drift toward Zachary and be picked up by a waiting boat. If the flames were normal, the tide was running in, and he was to release the barrels on the starboard side so they'd drift up onto Teignmouth beach, where a gang member would be waiting to collect them. The lights seen among the trees on the back of the Ness were due to the comings and goings of the gang, conferring with their leader.

"I could ask at this point if I've left anything unexplained," concluded Blackett wryly, "but I suspect you know the details as thoroughly as I do."

"Not at all," the young man protested. "I simply formed a hypothesis based on the facts at hand. I'm pleased that it proved to be correct."

Thomas Silver, listening silently, merely smiled around his pipe-stem.

"You're not the only one who's pleased, take it from me," Blackett said. "And if you ever have the inclination to prove any more hypotheses, lad, and put the finger on other villains, Scotland Yard would be more than glad to have you."

"I'll bear that in mind," Barham said politely, "but I'm afraid it wasn't my father's intention, when he sent me to university, for his son to become a policeman."

"No, very few fathers have that intention, come to that… Miss, another round of cider here, please!"

# The False Mr. Fordham

It was Owen Barham's custom, dating from when he was a boy, to pay a visit to his Uncle Peter's household toward the end of every summer.

Peter Burr and his family lived on a little island called St. Engelfrid, just off the coast of Dorsetshire. The island emerged from the waters of the Channel like a Christmas pudding: a round dome of earth, sparsely forested, which up 'til 1890 was of note only because of the small fishing village on its eastern side. In that year an artists' colony was established in the upper end of the village, with Owen Barham's uncle one of the first to take up residency there. The following year a retired showman by the name of Whittas built a hotel on the south end of the island, a magnificent white structure overlooking a splendid stretch of sand, which before long attracted the leading lights of entertainment and industry to its ornate rooms. A ferry travelled between the island and the mainland town of Swanage twice a day, bringing mail and visitors, to both the hotel and the artists' workshops. The rest of the villagers for the most part went on fishing for pilchard as they had always done, but few came to see that.

Burr was Owen's mother's brother, and something of a black sheep in the family. The Burrs and the Barhams were on the whole small, pale people, pressed down under the weight of generations of want and the hustle and bustle of the great metropolis. Peter Burr was a large, bearlike man, darker in complexion than any of his siblings, and similarly unlike them in taste and inclination. He had passed on his energy and his Falstaffian humour to his children, five sons and one daughter, and their home, with artists and models coming and going at practically all hours, was the nucleus of a convivial whirlwind. The boys for their part had long shown their familial affection by chaffing their younger, more scholarly cousin often and by testing his credulity with rags and yarns. These experiences in the end were not without worthwhile results: they had helped develop Barham's patience and steadfastness in the face of adversity, and the equanimity that was a large part of his character.

With this in mind, it was little wonder that Owen Barham was at first inclined to some skepticism regarding the comments his cousin Byron made to him one evening, as they were waiting in the front parlour for supper to be announced.

"Did you hear? There was a curious incident at the hotel this morning–just the sort of thing you tend to nose into, I'll wager. The front desk clerk saw one of the guests twice in short succession, and he did the same things both times."

Barham raised his eyebrows a fraction. "Surely that isn't unusual? He must encounter guests many times throughout the course of a day."

"Ah, but I see I haven't made myself clear. He spoke with this particular guest twice in twenty minutes, and the same exact interchange took place each time. The same conversation, the same actions, both times. He hasn't any explanation for it, and is halfway convinced there's something uncanny behind the affair." Byron Burr chuckled. "Our conversation about it didn't help, I daresay, with my maundering on about fetches, and doppelgangers, and the possibility of time unaccountably rolling backwards…"

"Is there any chance of your arranging a meeting with this clerk?" Barham asked, ignoring his cousin's allusions.

"I confess, you've whetted my interest. I'd like to hear the full story from him, if I can."

"Why not? He'll be at home this evening. We'll go round after supper and collect him, and then trot along to the pub and discuss the details over a pint or two."

Accordingly the pair went down the slanting streets into the village, once the family had dispersed from the evening's table, with the sun's rays dim and brazen among the shadows of the little houses. Before long they were joined by a third young man, and shortly afterward the trio seated themselves at a corner table in the public house, the windows of which looked out over the bay and the narrow boats lining its docks.

"Allow me to make formal introductions," Burr said. "Jules, this is my cousin, Owen Barham. Owen, this is Julian Poecock, who works at the front desk at the hotel."

The two shook hands. Poecock was sleek and well-dressed without being flashy, his shining black hair swept back from a pleasing face, with alert dark eyes, a narrow nose, and a rounded chin. He was a complete contrast to Barham, whose hair was the color of faded straw and whose pale blue eyes were contained behind round spectacles.

"I'm actually head clerk at the Whittas Hotel," Poecock said tolerantly, "though By always seems to manage to forget that. I've heard one or two things about you, I think–something of a detective, aren't you?"

"Not a professional one, by any means. I'm a student at University College in London."

"Is that so? Well, perhaps you can find some explanation for the events I experienced this morning nonetheless. I can't make any sense of them."

The other two made encouraging sounds, and Poecock, fortifying himself with a lengthy sip of ale, proceeded to relate his experience.

"To begin with, I should explain that we have a businessman staying at the hotel at present, one Grover H. Fordham. When he and his party arrived at the hotel a few days ago, he placed a briefcase in the hotel safe. This morning he came down to the front desk, a minute or two before nine o'clock I'd say, and asked to see the briefcase momentarily. We have a small alcove set aside for the guests to use for that purpose, to examine valuables left in our safekeeping, equipped with a little table, and pen and paper. I retrieved his case for him, and he placed it on the table and took a chequebook from it. I wasn't watching him, you understand, merely keeping nearby in case he should require any assistance, but I did happen to notice one or two things. He called to me shortly afterward and had me return the briefcase to the safe for him. At that time there was a signed cheque lying on the little table, which he placed in his pocket. When I returned from the inner office Mr. Fordham had passed out and was standing outside the hotel entrance, in conversation with another man. As I watched–in warm weather we keep the hotel doors standing open, so I could see them clearly–the man handed him a small package, and Mr. Fordham handed him what I assume was the folded cheque. They then turned along the promenade in the direction of the village, and passed out of my sight.

"Then, about twenty minutes later, it all happened again. I was standing at the front desk and looked up to see Mr. Fordham coming down the stairs from his room. It was like a reflection of the previous events, but through an old, wavy glass. He moved more slowly this time, his voice was thicker, his clothing was slightly disheveled. He came up to the desk, just as he had the first time, and asked for his briefcase. We went through the same actions as before. I brought him the case, he opened it and took out his chequebook–this time I was watching, though I tried not to let on that I was–and he made out a cheque and handed the briefcase back. Then he went out through the front doors, stood in front of the hotel for several minutes, looking this way and that, and eventually went off in the direction of the village.

"He returned to the hotel a little later in the morning, though I didn't see him myself, being away from the front desk momentarily. When I saw him again, it was noon, and he was coming down to the dining hall with his family. Everything appeared as usual then; they were talking together in normal tones, about commonplace things.

"There, that's my story, short as it is. If it means anything at all to you, I'd be pleased as Punch to hear it."

"I could make a guess myself," Burr said, "the most obvious one. Leaving aside any spectral explanations –"

"If you please," Poecock interjected drily.

"–I might inquire whether your businessman, the second time he came for his briefcase, bore the scent of spirits about him? The terrestrial sort, I mean. I assume you were close enough to him to detect the odor of the grape?"

Poecock rolled his eyes at the suggestion. "I'd sooner accept that 'William Wilson' was a true account, or that a man's shadow can detach itself from him and roam at will, than believe that Mr. Fordham is a sot. Not that he hasn't taken a drink or two on occasion, I've no doubt, but a more reserved and businesslike man you couldn't meet. And there was no suggestion of alcoholic vapours about his person this morning, on the first occasion or the second."

"Not to mention," added Owen Barham thoughtfully, "that twenty minutes would hardly have been enough time for him to have returned to his room by some roundabout route and managed to down enough intoxicating liquor to affect his movements and memory... There are other ways into the hotel apart from the front entrance, of course?"

"There's a narrow courtyard behind the hotel, where deliveries are brought and the dustbins are kept, though our guests are unlikely to venture back there. As well, there are some auxiliary exits on the west side of the building, but those are ordinarily kept locked."

Barham nodded and went on as though he hadn't heard. "Any poison or potion that could have affected him so strongly in such a short time would have left lingering signs. Yet I assume he appeared as normal when he returned to the hotel later in the morning?"

"I didn't see him, as I said, but the clerk who did, Deakins, acted as if Mr. Fordham's condition was perfectly ordinary. He certainly was his usual self by luncheon time."

"And had he changed clothing between the first time you saw him this morning and his second?"

"No, it all happened exactly the same way. The same suit and waistcoat, the same necktie–but slightly different at the same time, if you understand me."

"Was this the first odd incident involving Mr. Fordham that you know of?"

"The very first," Poecock said. "He and his family have stayed at the Whittas Hotel on multiple occasions, and nothing particularly worthy of mention happened on any of those other visits."

"What can you tell us about him?"

"Grover Fordham is a stock-broker of some note in the City, a big wheel on the Exchange. He's one of three brothers, all of whom are in business. His elder brother is on the board of directors of the London and South Western Railway, and his younger brother manages an up-and-coming insurance firm. His wife is from an old Northumberland family, and they have two children, a son and a daughter, both in their twenties. They vacation here each year with Mr. Fordham's widowed sister, Mrs. Festing-Airy, and her son Roger."

"You know a good deal about them, it seems," Barham said in mild surprise.

Poecock smiled. "Mr. Asbury, the hotel manager, encourages us to learn as much as we can about the guests, so as to make their stay as pleasant as possible. He even keeps personal notes on some of the more top-drawer guests."

"Can you describe the younger men to me–the nephew Roger, and the son?"

"The son, Hugo, resembles his mother and sister in appearance more than his father, being fair instead of brown-haired, but he's his father's child when it comes to business. He pores over the *Financial News* as ardently as Mr. Fordham does. The nephew, Roger, has the Fordham looks, dark brown hair and eyes, but hasn't the least interest in commerce, as far as I've seen."

"Do they normally choose this time of year to stay at your hotel?"

"Yes, as a rule."

"What are their rooming arrangements? Does Mr. Fordham sleep apart from his wife?"

"Yes, the family normally occupies a suite of rooms, so that each of them has a bed to themselves. Many gentlemen do that, you know, so as not to disturb their wives when business matters require a change in their routine."

Byron Burr, having listened to the discussion without interrupting up to that point, now thumped his empty glass upon the table. "What do you think, cousin?" he demanded. "Have you come to any conclusions yet?"

Barham glanced at him without replying, and Poecock said, "Why don't you refill our glasses, By? That's a good fellow."

Burr shrugged good-naturedly and headed for the bar. Barham asked, "Have you heard Mr. Fordham mention any certain type of stock, or anything else specific to his business, during this particular stay?"

"I haven't much chance to overhear the guests' conversations, not as much as I would if I worked in the dining hall, for instance, but I have heard him and his son speak of mining and processing metals on at least one occasion... By's right, isn't he? You have some notion of what this is about?"

The third young man, returning to their table with fresh glasses of ale in time to hear his name spoken, grinned widely. "Right, am I? Little wonder about that, if I do say so. What exactly is your idea, Owen?"

Owen Barham, perceiving that it was time to give the others some indications of his thoughts, straightened up in his chair.

"We can at least make some assumptions based on what we know," he said, "even if a definite conclusion isn't yet possible. To begin with, I believe the package you saw being exchanged outside the hotel is the key to all this. Its contents must fall into one of two categories, either a personal matter or a professional one. If it were something connected with the family, or merely a gift of some sort, I hardly think a man like this Mr. Fordham would arrange to have it brought to him in the middle of their holiday, and in such an offhand fashion. However, if it were something that related to his business, and that he wished to receive as soon as possible–perhaps even something that he wanted to keep his competitors in the dark about–he might well request it to be brought to the island. However, he could not have been absolutely certain that it would reach him here, or he would have made out his cheque for it in advance. Would you happen to know whether he telephoned the mainland, or received a wire, yesterday?"

Poecock shook his head. "We've had a pair of telephone cabinets installed in the hotel in recent years for the convenience of the guests, but I have no way of knowing who uses them, and when. And if he'd gone into the village to telephone or cable, well…"

"Never mind. We may be able to learn some details for ourselves later… Now, as to Mr. Fordham's double appearance this morning. For the present I think we may disregard any suggestions of the supernatural, and focus on more prosaic explanations. The most reasonable one is that some sort of impersonation was involved. But who was the impersonation meant to fool? Despite your interactions with the two Mr. Fordhams, I don't believe that you were the primary focus. I believe the man delivering the package was the target of the deception."

"If that's the case," Poecock said, "it looks to have failed. The first Mr. Fordham must have been the real one. He sounded like he should have, his manner and movements were correct, he signed his cheque with a firm and clear hand. The second one's voice was off, his movements were shaky, his clothing was haphazard–and his handwriting on the second cheque was barely legible. And all his pretence was for nothing, since the man he was expecting, and the package, were long gone by the time he exited the hotel."

"But what was it all about?" asked Burr. "Just what was in that so very important package, I wonder?"

His cousin asked, "Can you describe the man who was waiting outside the hotel?"

Poecock shook his head. "Not in any great detail. I don't claim to have gotten a very sharp look at him. He was a short, swarthy man in a dark suit. He could have been from Mexico, or Malta, or Mandalay, for all I know."

"But you did see the package he delivered clearly?"

"I could tell you the size and shape of it, roughly. I wasn't near enough to read any writing on it, or even tell whether there was writing on it."

"We may be able to dredge up some corroborating details," Barham said slowly, "but it would require some help on your part. I presume the hotel takes several newspapers, for the use of its guests?"

"Of course."

"And are they kept for a time, and not immediately discarded?... Then we may be able to find the information we're looking for in them. Could you arrange to let us into the hotel in the morning, for us to examine those papers?"

Early the following day, while a mere handful of the most fervent fresh-air enthusiasts were out on the wide silvery strand in front of the hotel, Owen Barham and Byron Burr crossed the weathered flagstones behind the grand white building and knocked at the door Julian Poecock had indicated. About five minutes later Poecock appeared, and with a few whispered words ushered them inside.

The rooms and hallways on the guests' side of the hotel might have been grandly memorable, but those on the staff side were narrow and decorated in utilitarian fashion. Poecock led them down a short corridor and around a corner to a storeroom filled with labelled boxes holding records and receipts, and to one side a double stack of newspapers, bound into bundles with twine.

"What are we looking for, exactly?" asked Burr, once they were alone.

"Any articles mentioning the subjects your friend overheard Mr. Fordham discussing," answered Barham. "Mining, or the processing of ore–we'll know it when we come across it."

Burr sighed and took out his clasp knife, and they began their perusal. It was not the activity he would have chosen to occupy his morning, but he was responsible for spurring his cousin to investigate the matter, and Barham expected him to do his part in the hunt.

It was not long, in the little airless room, before they shucked their coats and loosened their collars. It took them until nearly noon before, perspiring and ink-fingered, they found what Barham was looking for, in an edition dated almost two and a half weeks earlier. It was at the back of the financial section of one of the major London dailies, a brief report in the international column.

> THEFT AT MINING COMP. HEADQUARTERS
> The city of Santa Cruz de la Sierra, Bolivia, was abuzz with news of a theft last night in the offices of the San Cristobal Mining Company. A number of stock certificates, equal to five hundred shares in the firm, was taken from the executive safe of the director, Señor Manuel Diego y Olivera. A minor clerk in the company, one Juan Choque, is suspected of being responsible. Bolivian police have begun a search for Choque, and expect to soon recover…

Barham's first question, after reading the account, was not perhaps what his cousin might have expected.

"Remind me, please, exactly when the ferry travels between St. Engelfrid and the mainland? It's twice a day, I know…"

"Once in the morning," Burr replied, "and once in the evening. Ten o'clock in the a.m. and four in the p.m.–when it's on schedule."

"So that in order to meet Mr. Fordham in front of the hotel at nine o'clock yesterday morning, he would have had to have reached the island the previous afternoon, and sent some sort of message to signal his arrival… Could you find out if the hotel has a copy of *Lloyd's List,* and perhaps an atlas?"

Burr went out into the corridor to find his friend Poecock, and the pair returned shortly afterward with the requested items. Burr had followed his cousin's reasoning enough to bring the correct copy of the *List*, one from two days previous. Barham spread both out on the nearest level space, and turned to the map of South America while he scanned the columns for ships arriving in London that day.

"The journey here by train takes roughly two and a half hours, so counting back from the second ferry of the day brings us to one-thirty... Ah, here. The steamer *Pernambuco* reached London at twelve-thirty, after an eleven-day passage from Rio de Janeiro. From Santa Cruz de la Sierra to Rio de Janeiro would appear to be a difficult overland trek, and would certainly account for the rest of the time since the theft... The facts appear to support my hypothesis, but more proof would be needed than what we've been able to discover thus far. We could approach the police with this, but without more evidence of a link between these events..."

The only representative of the law on the island of St. Engelfrid was the village constable, named Dize, and for him to contact his superiors on the mainland would take much more than the few facts and suppositions Owen Barham had assembled.

"On the other hand," Barham said to Poecock, "if I'm correct, we may be able to put our hands on definite proof of a crime. It must be very nearly time for the guests to come down to luncheon... Though, if we're discovered, it could well mean the loss of your position here at the hotel."

"Let me worry about that," Poecock replied firmly. "If you can show me solid evidence that explains what I saw yesterday morning, it'll be enough for me."

Owen Barham nodded and outlined his plan, one detail of which made Poecock stare in amazement. The head clerk went off to surreptitiously borrow a set of master keys and survey the individuals filing into the dining hall. Before long he returned to the storeroom with the news that the Fordham party *in toto* was taking the noonday meal, whereupon the three young men hastened up the staff stairs at the back of the hotel to the room Barham had designated earlier, taking with them a certain package.

Barham and Poecock set to work searching the apartment, while Burr stood guard at the door. There were not many places where an article of any size might be hidden, and eventually they discovered what they were looking for at the bottom of the larger of the two trunks, a bulky envelope wrapped in stiff brown paper. Poecock called softly to his friend, and Burr left his post and brought his clasp knife to bear once more. The envelope, when shorn of its wrappings and slit open, proved to contain a thick stack of printed papers bearing the heading SAN CRISTOBAL MINING COMPANY. Barham gestured for the package they had brought upstairs with them, an envelope of similar size filled with sections of old newspaper, and wrapping it round with the brown paper, placed it where they had found the other. The three then tidied their surroundings, so as to leave no trace of their visit, and quitted the room forthwith.

The next evening they gathered round the corner table in the public house once more, but this time there was a fourth to their party–the local constable, a pear-shaped and sandy-haired fellow not too much older than them. They looked up at Constable Dize expectantly as he carefully deposited four glasses of foaming ale in the center of the table and settled into the remaining chair.

"You'll be a-wantin' to know 'ow matters turned out, I expect?" he said. "I travelled to Beaminster yesterday afternoon with the envelope you give me, that's Divisional 'Eadquarters, and presented it to my superior, Inspector Crown. It weren't long afore 'e called in 'is superior to 'ear the story as well. They've passed the facts, and the stock certificates, on to Scotland Yard. The stolen certificates'll be 'eaded back to Bolivia, and the Yard'll be a-keepin' a close eye on the Fordham 'ousehold for the near future. They'll catch one or another of 'em out eventually, I'm sure of that. Now I'd like to 'ear 'ow you come to discover just where those certificates were 'idden–a bit more of an explanation than the one you give me the first time, if you don't mind."

"And how you knew who had them," added Poecock. "From all I've seen and heard so far, he's the last one I would have named…"

Owen Barham gave a succinct description of the twin appearance of Grover Fordham two days prior for Constable Dize's benefit. It didn't take long to catch him up to speed, the story having already made the rounds of the village by then. Nonetheless Dize whistled under his breath.

"If 'twere me, I'd think I was being 'aunted, and go a-runnin' for the priest."

"I wasn't entirely convinced I hadn't been," Poecock admitted.

"If we put aside the involvement of supernatural agencies," Barham said, "the only answer is that it must have been a case of impersonation, aimed at deceiving the swarthy man in the dark suit, who came to deliver a certain package that morning. The impostor must have been someone who knew Grover Fordham very well, to know about the meeting in front of the hotel, to know what clothing he would have been likely to bring with him on this trip, and to have had access to Mr. Fordham's tailor, to order an identical suit made. The culprit could only have been one of the two young men in the party, either the son or the nephew. Based on the descriptions I was given, it seemed the nephew was far more likely to have impersonated Mr. Fordham."

Poecock shook his head. "It's hard to fathom. As far as anyone could tell, he hadn't the least interest in his uncle's business dealings."

"He may have given that impression," Barham said, "but the facts prove otherwise. You didn't tell me as much, but my suspicion is that the death of her husband left Mr. Fordham's sister in straitened circumstances, so that she and her son are now dependent on the kindnesses the rest of the family provide. When Roger Festing-Airy discovered his uncle's arrangements for the theft and subsequent delivery of the San Cristobal mining stock, he began making plans to seize the certificates for himself, no doubt intending to make his mark in the financial world."

"So which of 'em were the real Mr. Fordham?" asked Dize. "The first one, who said and did everything just so, or the second one, who carried on like a poor reflection of the first?"

"Certainly the first Mr. Fordham appeared to be the genuine article," replied Barham, "especially in comparison with the second, but it was his very correctness that made me suspect him. He signed the cheque he took from the briefcase carefully and clearly—but would the real Grover Fordham, brisk and businesslike, have taken the time to do that? Would he not rather have dashed off his signature quickly, as most of us tend to do?

"What I suspect happened is this: Roger Festing-Airy, learning of the planned delivery of the certificates to the hotel, made arrangements for his impersonation before the family ever left London, quite possibly with the assistance of his uncle's valet. He packed the duplicate suit of clothing as well as a dose of sleeping powders, which he managed to slip his uncle sometime during the evening preceding the delivery. His uncle thus indisposed, Festing-Airy rose that morning, dressed himself as the other man, and came downstairs to obtain a cheque from his uncle's briefcase, to which he had previously gained the combination. He met with the man we can now assume to be Juan Choque and took possession of the stolen certificates, then passed across the courtyard behind the hotel and up the rear stairs, which we ourselves later used, to his room, where he hid the package in his trunk and resumed his normal appearance.

"Twenty minutes later Grover Fordham awoke, his speech and movements dulled by the drug he had been given, and realising the time, he threw his clothes on and hurried down to keep the appointment he had made with Señor Choque. Not finding him outside the hotel, he no doubt came along to the village to attempt to locate him. Whatever happened after that, he was forced to keep the matter to himself, or risk revealing his orchestration of the theft at the San Cristobel Mining Company."

Byron Burr chuckled. "And in the end, after all their plotting, neither one of them gained a thing." He lifted his glass in a salute to Owen Barham. "Here's to you, cousin–you've proved it to my satisfaction–to our very own Great Detective!"

It was one of those September afternoons when, despite the crispness in the air, the sky was a clear blue and the sun surprisingly bright: the sort of weather, in fact, that was perfect for looking out at the great, moving world from behind glass. Thomas Beauclerk Silver was doing just that, his thumbs hooked in his waistcoat pockets, at the window of his little upstairs office in Whitefriars Street. Silver was a private enquiry agent, and in the entire span following his brief luncheon not a single client had appeared on his doorstep. So there he was, pacing about in boredom and watching the traffic moving up and down the thoroughfare.

A sound of footsteps on the stair, followed by the opening of his office door, caused him to turn from the window in surprise. He chuckled at the crabbed, sturdy figure in the doorway.

"Not a client, alas! And what's more ruinous for me and my reputation, you managed to slip in here without my being aware of it, despite my hanging about at this window. Come in, pull up a chair and rest your shoe leather–and tell me what brings you to this district."

Silver's visitor was an old friend, Inspector Gulledge of Scotland Yard, a grizzled and square-faced man in his middle years. Silver returned to the seat behind his desk as his friend settled into one of the secondhand leather chairs set aside for callers, removing his hat to reveal a head of bristly hair with a pronounced widow's peak. Gulledge declined the offer of a cigaret, and Silver fired up the long clay pipe that was his trademark as the inspector launched into his story.

"You've heard about the Hampstead murder, no doubt?"

"Only what I've been reading in the papers. An Italian nobleman, stabbed under mysterious circumstances, motive and identity of the killer unknown…"

"Yes. The press has taken to calling it the Hampstead Heath affair, despite the fact that the house where it happened isn't on the Heath itself, but only faces it across Branch Hill Road. At any rate, I've been spending the afternoon following up on the only two suspects we've been given, and little enough good that's done…"

Gulledge went on with a grim expression, describing the case for his friend, including the steps he had taken thus far and his lack of results. When he had finished Silver shook his head in puzzlement.

"It most certainly is a conundrum. I couldn't begin to suggest where the answer might lie–not that you came here expecting me to. However, it strikes me that there is someone who might have a glimmer or two. You recall my friend Owen Barham, the student at University College?"

"Oh yes, the young man from the Valdonato case."

"Among others. I've no doubt he'd be willing to spare some time to listen to the facts, if you can stand to tell the whole tale again. Although, knowing him, he'll probably want to look over the scene of the crime himself. Would that be possible?"

"Why not? And you'll want to come along, of course…"

The Saturday following, Inspector Gulledge, with a somewhat bemused constable behind the wheel, collected Silver and Owen Barham from the latter's lodgings in Torrington Square and travelled up the length of Hampstead Road to the southwestern corner of the Heath. They parked the car on the open side of the road, and the

Four men climbed out and looked across at the large houses opposite. Gulledge indicated one that was narrower than its neighbours, of pale pink brick with tall white pillars bracketing the front door.

"This, gentlemen, is the house where the murder occurred," he said. "Before we go inside and get into the details of the crime, I want you to get a clear picture of the setting. As you can see, the property is surrounded on three sides by tall hawthorn hedge. Attempting to gain access from any of the adjoining properties would take considerable effort, not to mention being more than unpleasant, and we found no signs that anyone had tried to do so on the day of the crime. That leaves us with the normal means of entry: through the front gate, through the side door onto the courtyard, or through the tradesmen's entrance at the rear of the house. To be clear, there are two sets of French doors on the left side of the house, but those are no longer used for entry or exit, particularly since a wide herbaceous border was put in place along that side by the previous owner. Anyone making use of those doors would leave footprints in the soft earth of the border, and we found no such footprints. Neither did we find evidence that any of the windows had been tampered with.

"Note the property to the right, the one with the wide expanse of lawn behind its low fence. There is in the district a man named Bowfry, who offers his services as gardener and groundskeeper to those householders who happen not to employ such on a permanent basis. He and his eldest son were engaged in trimming that lawn on the day in question, and spent the afternoon pushing their cylinder mowers back and forth across it–a task that was by no means brief, as you can imagine, but which afforded them a full view of the victim's home. That particular day—Wednesday last—was overcast, not sunny and clear like today, but the weather presented no hindrance to their view. They both swear that there were two visitors, and only two visitors, to the house that afternoon. But we'll get to that in a moment. Come along."

Gulledge led them across the road, through the front gate and up the path to the front door of the house, taking a ring of keys from his pocket as he went.

"The house is empty at present," he said, swinging open the wide, rose-coloured door. "The servants have taken temporary lodgings in Saffron Hill, and the victim was the only resident."

He led them down the long entrance hall, with its pillars and floor tiles of marble veined faintly with pink and blue. The constable, who had probably never been inside a house of such distinction, gazed about him speechlessly; Thomas Silver's deep-set dark eyes swept over his surroundings thoughtfully; and Owen Barham trailed along behind, apparently woolgathering, with his hands in his trouser pockets and his pale eyes distant behind his round spectacles, but nonetheless attentive to all his companions were saying.

The main hall ended at a second, smaller corridor that cut across the width of the house. Of the rooms opening off that corridor, Inspector Gulledge stepped, not to the door directly in line with the entrance, but to the one to the right of it, a corner room.

"This is the study, the room where the victim was killed," Gulledge said, with his hand on the doorknob. "This corridor we're in leads to a portico in the courtyard, while around the corner another hallway runs back to the kitchen and the rear entrance. Keep those points in mind, if you please."

He swung open the door, and they crowded in on his heels. The study was sparsely but tastefully decorated: a large black leather-topped desk and an accompanying chair of burgundy leather, a small filing cabinet with a bust of Garibaldi, a pair of spindly Regency-style chairs for guests, and landscapes by Castaldo and Corot. The desktop was well supplied with pens, inkwells, paper, envelopes, and all the other requisites for business.

"The victim," began the inspector, taking out his notebook for reference, "was Don Alessio Enzo, the Marchese di Sipicciano di Costaguti. There are several of these Italian names in the case, and each of them a mouthful. The Marchese was in England supposedly to strengthen ties of industry between this country and his homeland, particularly in the areas of steel manufacture and chemical production. For household staff he surrounded himself with individuals from his native district in Italy.

"At approximately ten minutes to four o'clock that Wednesday afternoon the Marchese was discovered by his butler slumped across his desk, dead. He had retired to the study after a brief midday meal to review his correspondence and compose his itinerary for the upcoming month. The butler, Amedeo Repetto by name, had come to the study to confer with his master about arrangements for afternoon tea, a habit the Marchese had taken up during his time here.

"Subsequent examination showed that the victim had been stabbed through the left ear, the blow piercing his brain and his vascular artery and causing him to bleed to death in a fairly short time. The weapon used, according to the pathologist's report, was a narrow blade approximately twenty centimetres in length. It was not found at the scene. The Marchese did have a thin steel letter opener on his desk, a little shorter than the size mentioned, but it was free of any traces of blood. There were marks on the victim's left sleeve indicating that the killer wiped the weapon clean on the body before departing.

"My first task was to determine who was in the house that afternoon, beginning with the servants. The Marchese's private secretary, Piettro Parodi, had been dispatched to Harringay after luncheon to iron out the details of a business contract, and was there during the entire time in question. He, at least, is completely out of the case.

"The butler claims to have been upstairs all afternoon, aside from two exceptions, which I'll come to at length. At his master's instructions, he had been replacing the curtains in the various rooms, originally of a light linen, with something heavier. Ordinarily he would have been assisted by the maid, but she had been dismissed several days earlier.

"The chauffeur, Luca Battilana, was in the courtyard beside the house, cleaning the Marchese's two large touring cars.

"The cook, Fiorenza Bruzzone, was seated outside the study in the rear hallway. There's a chair placed there especially for her, one large enough and comfortable enough to accommodate her frame, where she could easily hear a summons from her master but also make her way directly to the kitchen when needed. She spent the time knitting; she showed me the scarf she'd made, all reds and browns and oranges, very autumnal.

"Apart from the servants, the Marchese had two visitors that afternoon. The first was Mr. Percival Coffing, one of the managers of the Ditton Works foundry, and he had an appointment with the Marchese at 1.30. He arrived on time, and the butler came downstairs to admit him to the study. The ensuing conversation did not proceed smoothly; there was a sharp outburst on the part of Mr. Coffing, according to the butler, and he banged the study door upon his departure.

"About forty-five minutes later another visitor arrived and pressed repeatedly on the bell. He did not have an appointment; he gave his name as Ambrose Bramwell, said that his business was personal, and pushed his way inside before the butler could stop him. Upon learning that the Marchese was in his study, he burst into the room. What followed was a heated exchange with the victim, and after giving vent to his feelings Mr. Bramwell strode out of the house in a rage.

"To some extent all this is attested to by the Bowfrys, whom I mentioned earlier. They testified that they could see the butler moving about at one window after another during the afternoon, that the chauffeur spent the entire time at work in the courtyard, and that only two vehicles, those belonging to Mr. Coffing and Mr. Bramwell, stopped in front of the house that afternoon.

"I next located and interviewed the Marchese's two visitors. According to Mr. Coffing, the Marchese had indicated a desire on previous occasions to broker a partnership between a pair of companies back in Italy and the Ditton Works, and Coffing was flabbergasted to discover that not only was this not to be the case, but that the man had been carefully noting the foundry's production methods and trade secrets and conveying them to his countrymen to provide them with an unfair advantage in the international market. When confronted with this the Marchese gave vent to certain provocative remarks, causing Mr. Coffing to vow to 'wring his bloody Latin neck' should they ever meet in future. He swears, however, that the Marchese was alive when he left him, and the testimony of both the butler and Mr. Ambrose Bramwell confirms this.

"Mr. Bramwell is on the board of directors of the United Alkali Company. It appears the Marchese met Mr. Bramwell's sister during a dinner hosted by the company and pursued the acquaintance, to the point of escorting Miss Bramwell to questionable night-clubs and introducing her to the use of cocaine. The Marchese was a relatively young man, not yet forty, and had something of a reputation as a rake and a roué. His dalliance with Miss Bramwell was not at all unusual for him. Upon receiving Bramwell's warning to stop seeing his sister or face the unpleasant consequences, the Marchese merely replied in an insulting manner. Bramwell admits to being driven to the point of threatening violence, but like Percival Coffing, insists that the nobleman was alive when he departed.

"The butler agrees with Mr. Bramwell's statement, and in fact the Exchange has record of a trunk call being placed from the house at around two-forty. The caller identified himself as the Marchese di Sipicciano di Costaguti, and asked to be connected with a number in Genoa, Italy.

"According to the staff, there were no other visitors to the house that afternoon. The butler denies admitting anyone apart from Mr. Coffing and Mr. Bramwell, and the chauffeur says that no other vehicles approached the residence.

"I've tried my best to consider all the possibilities. The medical evidence appears to clear both visitors; if we imagine one of them carrying in a concealed weapon and somehow stabbing the Marchese in the ear unawares–I know, it boggles the mind–he could not have survived long enough to engage in a second heated conversation or to place that seven-minute telephone call at two-forty. In spite of that, I contacted friends and business acquaintances of both Mr. Coffing and Mr. Bramwell, and they substantiated the facts behind both men's stories."

"Are you certain the telephone call–" began Silver, but his friend cut him off with a curt gesture.

"I thought of that, too," Gulledge said. "It took the assistance of an officer at the Yard fluent in Italian, but I managed to contact the party in Genoa who received the call. It was indeed the Marchese who placed it, and he referred to details only he would have known.

"This, then, is the question I'm left with: how could the killer have gotten into the house and the study without anyone being aware of it? You've heard about the condition of the outside of the house, and the testimony of the Bowfrys, but still I put all that aside and considered the room itself. You can see there are two doors, the one that faces the front of the house, and the second, which opens onto the side corridor beside Signora Bruzzone's chair. She speaks hardly two words of English, and I had to have the butler's aid in questioning her, but when asked she said definitely that no one passed her the entire time, and she heard no one entering the study by either door. I don't doubt her, either: you walked through that front hall, with its marble tiles, and I can't believe anyone could approach from that direction without his footsteps echoing throughout the house."

Silver appeared about to speak, but Gulledge held up a hand to avert it. "I even had a local builder in here, to inspect the room and take measurements. There are no secret passages or sliding panels to admit some mysterious malefactor. Now–you had a thought?"

"Only to ask if there were any signs of a struggle, or defensive wounds?"

"None. Yes, it indicates that the Marchese was taken by surprise, possibly by someone he didn't consider threatening. Another reason to strike Coffing and Bramwell from the list of suspects.

"I've considered the likelihood of some sort of conspiracy, as well. Considering the victim's nationality, was this the act of some Camorra or Black Hand assassin? Had the Marchese's staff been cowed into silence by those responsible, or had they themselves joined in a pact to slay their employer?"

Silver regarded him with a humorous glint in his dark eyes. "However, considering the story they stick to…"

"Exactly. If they were involved in the crime in some way, why insist that the Marchese was alive after his second visitor departed? It would have been far simpler for them to have said they found him dead on the heels of Mr. Bramwell's exit, and it would have been their word against his, considering the circumstances.

"At this point I'm willing to grasp at any explanation. The Marchese's killer somehow gained access to the scene without leaving any trace of his presence, bringing and taking away whatever weapon he used, and with his motive a complete blank. How? Did he drop down out of the sky from an airship or a hot air balloon?"

"Shades of Jules Verne," murmured Silver.

"Even in that case the murderer would've been seen. I leave it to you–what sense can anyone make of this situation?"

In response Silver glanced over at Owen Barham with raised eyebrows, and Gulledge turned in that direction as well. The young man's response was not quite what any of the others expected. He lifted his head at the lull in the conversation, his blue eyes still dreaming behind his spectacles, and addressed the inspector.

"You haven't said anything about the maid," he said simply. "Why was she dismissed?"

Gulledge shook himself with some irritation. "You really imagine she could have something to do with this crime? As far as we know she was nowhere near Hampstead at the time."

"I think that area of the case could at least stand closer examination."

"Is that all, lad? You haven't anything more concrete to tell me?"

Barham shrugged apologetically. "The affair seems fairly straightforward, from everything you've told us, but the motive is utterly obscure. I strongly suspect you'll uncover it once you delve into the circumstances behind the maid's dismissal. But if not, if you can find no clear connexion between the two events, then I'll gladly tell you what my thoughts are, and you can determine for yourself whether they're helpful."

More than that the young man was unwilling to say. They quit the murder house and climbed into the inspector's official car again, and drove south out of Hampstead with Gulledge in a darker humour than he had begun the day.

The next evening he met with Silver and Owen Barham once more, this time in the latter's quarters in Torrington Square. The three of them sat around the postage-stamp-sized table in the young man's cramped sitting room, sampling black tea and biscuits. Gulledge, his mood a good deal lighter than when they had last seen him, tilted his ladder-backed chair backward so that it teetered on its rear feet.

"You were right about the maid," he said to Owen Barham. "The investigation is finished now, at least the Yard's part in it, and it's been handed on to the Solicitor-General's Office. The woman confessed everything once we confronted her. This time I took along the officer from the Yard who speaks Italian, so there was no trying to slip anything past us."

"The maid?" asked Silver, who was trying to follow this exposition. "You managed to locate her, then?"

"Eh? Oh, no, not the maid, the cook–Signora Bruzzone. She killed her master with one of her knitting needles, and then wiped it off and resumed her knitting as cool as you please, leaving the butler to discover Don Alessio dead at his desk.

"The motive for the crime was the Marchese's treatment of the maid, who was Signora Bruzzone's daughter. It seems the Marchese seduced the girl, and when it became obvious that she was with child, he sacked her. Having no other family here in England, and the

Marchese's stay in the country a temporary one in any case, Signora Bruzzone paid to book passage for her daughter on a boat back to their district in Italy. The day following her arrival in their home village, feeling the shame and disgrace of her position, the girl made her way into nearby Genoa, to the office of a disreputable back-alley doctor who was willing to perform a certain operation. The operation had disastrous consequences; the girl died on his doorstep; her mother received a letter from their family in Italy telling the heart-wrenching tale the day before the Marchese's death.

"With all of this brewing inside her, Signora Bruzzone took her customary seat outside the study that Wednesday, only to learn that her master was still up to his lecherous ways. She could hear what Ambrose Bramwell said during his brief visit, especially since he was shouting in the Marchese's face, and her anger and grief became too much to bear."

"She could understand more English than she let on, then," said Thomas Silver.

"Right. She marched into the study while the Marchese was making his telephone call, and as he replaced the receiver in its cradle she plunged the needle into his brain and avenged her daughter's death."

Barham nodded. "Given the circumstances you described, that was the only explanation that appeared possible. You asked the cook whether anyone had passed her and entered the study, and she truthfully said no one had; you never asked her whether she committed the murder."

" 'I will meet them as a bear that is bereaved of her whelps, and will rend the caul of their heart…'" quoted

Silver soberly, and then chuckled. "Just imagine—one simple question, and the case could have been sewn up on your first visit to the Marchese's house. Something to keep in mind the next time, old cock."

Gulledge, considering the various replies at the tip of his tongue to be beneath the dignity of a representative of Scotland Yard, contented himself with dropping his chair to the floor with a *thump* and rummaging protractedly through his pockets for a nonexistent item.

On an early October evening, while a brisk wind sent leaves and rubbish skittering up the broad avenue toward the statue of George III astride his horse, five men sat in the warmth of their club with their heads close together. The previous evening there had been a singular incident in the club depository–an incident not particularly unusual, perhaps, among the myriad throngs of London, but unexpected enough in its circumstances to have sparked a blaze of conjecture among the club's members.

Their club was the Saturnian, its society open to those with a shared interest in historical subjects. On its first floor, off the main hallway, was located a depository, where treasures of great antiquity or historical significance were kept for individuals to ponder at their leisure. The club steward had been discovered, in the hour before midnight, stretched insensate on the floor of the depository before a certain ancient chest, his sightless eyes turned to the ceiling and one arm flung out in the direction of a statue of St. Guthlac. This sudden incapacitation of one who had theretofore professed the halest of health, and the curious details attendant upon it, made a potent nursery for more and more extravagant theories.

After listening to the latest such theory from his confreres, the noted actor Simeon Vale, whose finely-chiseled profile had decorated show-bills from the West End to the West Country, snorted in disbelief.

"Nonsense," he said pleasantly. "As William of Ockham was fond of remarking to friends and neighbours, 'Plurality should not be posited without necessity'–or, in language that you and I might understand, 'The simplest explanation is often the correct one.' Can you honestly avow that a celestial visitation so awe-inspiring as to strike poor Withrow into instant unconsciousness is the simplest explanation–particularly occurring in a gentlemen's club in St. James's?"

Henderson, who was both a financier and a staunch believer in Intelligences from Beyond, fingered the black ribbon dangling from his spectacles sulkily and made no reply.

"It needn't have been a flight of seraphs, you know," said De Bow, turning his wineglass in his long, artistic fingers. "Remember that his hand was pointing at the statue of Guthlac when he was found–and we know the sort of visitors that old hermit received in his island hovel. Devils fearsome of visage and raucous of tongue, filling almost the entire space betwixt earth and heaven with their shrieks."

"In sibilant speech, in the Celtic language of the peasants haunting that wild district," murmured Rutherford, stroking his bottle-brush beard absently.

Godby lifted his moon face and spoke drily, like the civil servant he was. "Let's not get carried away by our orthodox upbringings, gentlemen. The Utgartha Chest, in front of which unfortunate Withrow was found, comes from a different tradition entirely. Not for those doughty Teutons the cloven-hoofed and scarlet-hued tormentors of the Christian faith; their nightmares were comprised of frost giants, trolls, and other such monstrous grotesques. Could he have been caught in some dread clash between opposing forces of deviltry?"

Vale sighed and restrained himself from rolling his eyes. "Or perhaps there's a far more prosaic explanation.

Perhaps Withrow suffered an abrupt apoplectic fit or a sudden brain storm…"

"In a man of such good health as he?" retorted Rutherford. "I can hardly imagine what stresses might have arisen in the night, in the quiet of an empty club, to prompt such an attack. And you mustn't forget the writing on the lid of the chest. Surely no humdrum explanation can account for the presence of Ogham script above his senseless body."

"Minoan," Henderson spoke up gruffly. "There is no doubt in my mind that the words are a form of ancient Minoan–which, as everyone knows, was the root of the great Atlantean tongue."

"I beg to differ," said Godby with some asperity. "The writing on the lid of the Utgartha Chest is most certainly cuneiform."

Vale was on the verge of throwing up his hands in a gesture of frustration, when De Bow's ironic chuckle stopped him short.

"You simply must submit, old man. We have no way of knowing what went on here last night. Why not let these fine fellows spin their gossamer fancies?"

Henderson, stung by this, glared and began, "Do you seriously deny–"

Simeon Vale ignored him and regarded De Bow thoughtfully. "There may be a way we can discover the cause of Withrow's fit, at that. My nephew, as you may recall, is sitting at University College, and he's spoken on occasion of a fellow student who's gained a bit of a reputation as a solver of puzzles. I suggest that we call in this young man, and see what sense he can make of the situation."

The suggestion was not met with immediate approval by the others, but before long Vale's masterful personality won out, and he stalked off to the telephone cabinet to call his nephew. About thirty minutes later he met the two young men on the front steps of the club and ushered them in to meet the others.

One lad was long-legged and wavy-haired, a manifest echo of his uncle in certain gestures and expressions. The other was pale and slender, with brushed-back blond hair and light-coloured eyes behind round spectacles.

"Gentlemen, my nephew Sebastian, and his friend Owen Barham... Sebastian, Owen, may I introduce Messieurs Henderson, Rutherford, De Bow, and Godby..."

Vale settled the visitors into comfortable seats and swiftly outlined the question at hand. His nephew laughed briefly when he had finished and exchanged glances with his friend.

"I'm sorry, Uncle, I don't mean to be rude, but it's a bit of a rum go, this. If I follow you, you want Owen to either prove that there was a supernatural agency at work last night–a thing which, by its very nature, has to be taken on faith–or prove a negative, that there was no such agency afoot. And that's going to be a very tricky thing indeed to prove. Absence of evidence is not evidence, and all that."

Vale, nettled, leaned back and took a firm grip on the arms of his chair. "Then it's just as well that we're not discussing a scientific theorem, isn't it? Look, my boy, this is patently a club, and not a commercial laboratory. All I'm asking is for your friend to have a peep round, and see if he notices anything that might lead him to some conclusions."

"I'm willing to look into the matter," said Barham quietly, "but has anyone thought of paying a visit to this Mr. Withrow, and asking him what occurred?"

The men glanced guiltily at one another. It was one thing to sit in the comfort of their club, weaving theories with fine liquor and tobacco at hand, but it had not entered their minds to venture forth to the bedside of the stricken steward and ask him for the facts.

Vale stood decisively. "By all means, let's go to him. Withrow was taken to Westminster Hospital. We should be able to get in to see him despite the hour."

The other club members declined to accompany him, for one reason or another, and Vale had the doorman ring for a taxi. At the front door his nephew bid them farewell, leaving only Vale and Barham.

"It's getting late, Uncle, and Owen here can always give me the full yarn some other time. Good hunting!"

Westminster Hospital was not at all distant. The short trip took them past George III and then Charles I at Charing Cross, kings marching eternally in bronze, and then down the length of Whitehall among the silently staring government buildings, to a crenellated brick structure at the foot of the Abbey. They were well outside any visiting hours, but Vale exercised his silver tongue on the matron on duty and they found themselves being escorted up to the second-floor ward where Withrow was resting.

"Mind you," she said, before opening the door, "you're not to tire him out. After a head injury like that, the patient needs rest more than anything else."

Vale promised solemnly that they would not tax the infirm man more than necessary, and they went in. The club steward was a stocky man, his face pale against the pillows and a lank forelock drooping over the bandage that wound like a crown around his head.

"Vale! What are you doing here? Is there-is there trouble at the club?"

"Not at all, old sport. Just came to see how you were faring, don't y'know, and what caused this calamity. Whatever were you doing in the treasury room last evening?"

Withrow lifted one hand tentatively to his bandage. "To tell you the truth, Vale... well, fact of the matter is, I can't remember. Not a jot, don't you see. Last thing I recall is working in my rooms and the telephone ringing–but what happened after I picked up the receiver, and who was on the line... it's all a complete blank to me. Next thing I knew, I was waking up here."

"Well, nothing to worry about, nothing to worry about. Your brother has the club well in hand, so you get your rest, and you'll be right as rain before you know it."

They excused themselves, and as they stepped into the corridor came face-to-face with the matron, who had brought the attending surgeon with her. He was a tall, narrow man with a harassed expression, who introduced himself as Dr. Felgate.

"I trust you gentlemen did not worry the patient needlessly? Quite irregular, this calling on patients outside of hours."

"We left him calm as a babe, I assure you," said Vale smoothly. "And our visit this evening is not without purpose. This young man is a detective, investigating the cause of Mr. Withrow's condition."

"Another one?... I would have supposed you would have communicated with Inspector Benedict, who was here earlier, instead of bothering the patient a second time, but then I am not conversant with the ways of the police. Have you learned what you needed?"

"Very little, I'm afraid," Vale replied after a startled pause. "Mr. Withrow seems to be suffering from a loss of memory."

"Yes, the condition is common with head injuries of that kind. The immediate time period leading up to the incident is often a blank. His memory will return in time, however, at least in part."

"Of course. I understand he struck his head on the floor in falling, but our real wonder is, what circumstances caused the fall in the first place? I don't suppose you have any medical insight into that question?"

Felgate stared at him. "You really haven't spoken with Inspector Benedict, then." He cleared his throat self-consciously. "Seeing as you're on the case as well, so to speak, I don't suppose it can do any harm to tell you gentlemen what I told him. Mr. Withrow did not hit his head in a fall. He was struck a blow on the back of the head with what appears to have been some sort of curved object. Upon realising that, I felt it my duty to apprise the police…"

"Er, certainly. Quite right, Doctor. Well, we shan't take up any more of your time. Good evening."

As they headed down the stairs to the entrance Vale muttered, "This certainly paints a new perspective on the situation. A blow to the head!"

"Mr. Withrow mentioned that he was working in his rooms before the incident," Barham said. "They're located somewhere on the club premises, I take it?"

"Yes, he lives there, in fact. Has his office and private rooms on the third floor of the building."

"With a telephone connexion on that floor?"

"Right-ho. I told him the truth, you know. His brother's come down from Grimsby to manage the club in his absence, and has the place humming along as usual... Well, if the doctor can't shed light on the circumstances, I know who can. Mannering, the fellow who found Withrow in the treasury. He was at the club earlier, and should be there still."

They returned to the Saturnian, and found Mannering in the club bar. He dabbed the foam from his clipped grey moustache and grinned.

"You'd like to hear the story again, eh? Feel as though I've told it a thousand times since yesterday. Ah, I haven't met your young friend, have I? Delighted, delighted. Well, gents, if you must know, it's all on account of some property I'm putting on the market in Mayfair. Had the paperwork with me last evening, and it wasn't until I was at home, at almost eleven o'clock, that I discovered I'd left one of the pages behind in the club library. Of course the club was well shut up by then–as a matter of fact, Wednesdays are the early day, as I don't have to tell you, Vale; the doors close promptly at nine–but I 'phoned Withrow to fetch the paper and bring it down to the front door. Had to have it in hand, you see. I had a meeting with my broker first thing this morning, and I hadn't time to wait for the club to open to retrieve it.

"Well, he agreed readily enough, but once I was here, standing on the front steps with the taxi waiting, he didn't show. Finally I took out my key—as a member of the club committee, young man, I have keys to the front and rear entrances—and let myself in. Rather an old mausoleum with the lights out and no one about, and I whistled a little tune to lift my spirits. I started up to the library, on the second floor, but I noticed a light coming from the depository, and headed for that instead. Found Withrow sprawled on his back on the floor, with a cracked head, utterly insensible. Only thing to do was to 'phone for the local doctor, and he had Withrow taken to hospital straightaway."

"Would he have had any reason to be in the depository at that time of night?" asked Barham.

"None that I can see. The room is cleaned once a week by the charwomen, and apart from them the displays are rarely ever handled. There's simply no need."

"Did anything appear to be missing, or disturbed, in the room when you reached it?"

"Everything was as usual. Can't imagine what he was doing in there."

"Did you see, or hear, signs of anyone else on your way to the depository?"

"Not a jot. Of course the staff would have all gone by then. Even if some of the kitchen help were still present, well, the kitchen's in the basement, and they'd have had no clue what was going on up here."

"You mentioned that the club closes early on Wednesday evenings. Is that the only night that occurs?"

"Yes, Withrow likes to have one evening a week to himself, gives him time to pore over the books and what not. Other days members stay as late as ten or ten-thirty before toddling off home."

"So his routine would be common knowledge among the members... Would you be able to show me the rear entrance to the club? Or at least tell me this–can it be seen from the front entrance?"

"Afraid not. The main hall comes to an end at a cross corridor, at a set of double doors, and if you pass through those and turn right, then wend your way round to the left again, you'll reach a hallway that opens onto a courtyard leading to Carlton House Terrace."

"And the rear door takes a similar type of key to the front?"

"That's right. It's a standard door, and kept locked after hours. You'd need the key to unlock it from the inside or from the outside."

Barham nodded and turned to Simeon Vale. "I'd like to see the depository now, if it isn't against the club rules."

"Not at all," the actor said heartily, and the three of them went along to the room where Withrow had been found. It was a square room with a row of waist-high shelving around its four sides holding various antiquities, while more notable (and lighter) objects hung on pegs on the walls. A small writing table and chair, with paper and ink and other essentials, was placed in the center of the room for those members who might wish to examine a particular object closely and make notes. Mannering indicated the Utgartha Chest, before which the prone club steward had been found.

The chest was about three feet long by a foot and a half deep, its oaken surface carved with figures representing hunters casting arrows after boars and stags–or perhaps some scene from Germanic mythology–and its corners girded with iron stays. The lid stood open, and on its inside could be seen a series of scratches or short cuts, appearing to begin on the right and run to the left, where the impressions were deepest.

"Is the lid usually left open like this?" asked Barham.

"On the contrary," replied Mannering. "There's nothing of particular note on the inside of the chest, except some age-old dust, and it was empty when it was uncovered in that field in Lower Silesia, so there'd be nought to gain by peering inside."

Owen Barham studied the scratches in the lid once more and then began to pace around the parquet floor. A short distance away he stooped abruptly and straightened up holding a small, triangular piece of metal, moderately sharp on two sides and jagged on the third.

"What's that?" asked Vale. "A bit of knife blade, is it?"

Barham, not heeding him, had lifted his head and was gazing at the relics hanging on the walls. On the west wall was a crossed pair of swords, and he stepped up before these.

"Ah, yes," said Mannering, "the Oakshott swords, believed to date from the final years of Edward III's reign. Found at the bottom of a refuse heap, outside a small farm in Hampshire."

"Could we have the swords down?" asked Barham.

Vale, the tallest of the three, reached up and brought down the frontmost of the two swords. Its tip was missing, and the piece in Barham's hand, when he held it up, fit the broken edge exactly. Vale gave vent to an exclamation of surprise.

"Someone took this weapon down, broke off the end of it, and then replaced it on the wall? Whatever for? Have you an explanation?"

"Those are the key questions, don't you agree?" Barham responded with a smile. "Why return the sword to its place, when it was damaged? Why open an empty chest?"

"You think this is what was used to carve the writing into the lid, then?"

Barham held the broken piece up to the lid of the Utgartha Chest. "I would say so, though to be frank, I don't believe this is any kind of message at all. Now, if I'm correct…"

Following the next thought in his mind, he bent his head to examine the items arranged along the shelf beneath the Oakshott swords. He stopped in front of a cup of some dark metal and picked it up, turning it toward the light.

"Oh, yes, the Eisenstadt Goblet—" began Mannering.

"With all respect," Vale returned sharply, "will you contain yourself?"

Realising he still held the sword in his hand, he restored it to its place on the wall sheepishly and watched Owen Barham. The young man held the goblet up for Vale's inspection and pointed to some dull stains along the rim.

"What do you think? Could this be blood?"

"Blood?" Vale repeated, trying to comprehend the significance of what he was hearing. "So you think someone bashed poor old Withrow on the bean with that cup, managing meanwhile to also break the tip off one of the Oakshott swords, and then put everything back in its place? Why on earth go to the trouble?"

"Exactly. There's only one plausible explanation for taking such a step."

"And the identity of this mysterious assailant? Have you any notion about that?"

Before Barham could respond, two more members of the club, Henderson and De Bow, came through the doorway with fresh news.

"We've been invaded," De Bow announced archly. "Have you heard? There's an inspector of police closeted with Maurice Withrow, no doubt combing through every detail of his brother's role as club steward."

"It's probably the same one who visited Withrow at hospital," returned Vale. "We seem to be dancing around each other. I would never have dreamed this was a police case, until I heard the doctor's description of Withrow's injury."

"Oh, yes. And has your distinguished guest discovered anything here in the depository?"

"Yes, have you learned what happened here last night?" echoed Henderson.

"We've at least learned that there was nothing unearthly at hand," Vale said tartly. "From the available evidence, it appears there was a second–"

He broke off as another pair of men appeared in the depository doorway. One was Maurice Withrow, who shared his brother's square jowls but had a sharply receding hairline in place of his sibling's full head of hair. The second man was heavier, with a round belly and his hands plunged deep in the pockets of his tweed overcoat. He regarded them keenly from beneath the brim of his hat.

"This is Inspector Benedict, from the Canon Row Station," said Withrow. "He's here to look into what happened in the club last night. I'm sure you gentlemen will give him every assistance."

"Assuredly so," responded De Bow. "Whatever we can do to help find the person who cracked poor Withrow over the head."

Owen Barham, still gripping the goblet, stared at the men, then stepped close to his host. "Mr. Vale, the men you introduced me to earlier–are they all members of the club committee?"

Vale looked at him in surprise at the seemingly inconsequent question. "Yes, all of them. Matter of fact, I'm the only one you've met this evening who isn't one."

Barham nodded, and lifting his voice said, "Inspector, might I have a word with you? I need to explain some things…"

The Canon Row officer stepped aside with him, and as the young man spoke earnestly to him in a low tone, holding up the Eisenstadt Goblet to punctuate his comments, Benedict's expression changed from a faint, tolerant amusement to a solemn determination. The inspector nodded briskly as their conversation drew to a close, and for the first time the others could hear his voice clearly.

"Quite right," he said. "If you have your facts correct, that may be the best solution. I'll have to speak with my superiors about it, of course."

The postscript to the Saturnian Club matter, as far as Owen Barham was concerned, came exactly a week later, as he was walking between classrooms at University College. He glanced up from the path to see Sebastian Vale fall into step beside him.

"What ho! Thought you'd like to know the little mystery at my uncle's club was resolved last night. The police johnnies set a watch on the club treasure room, and when a group of three men sneaked in and began to scoop up the various historical gewgaws they bundled in and collared the lot of 'em. The would-be thieves were all wearing black silk masks, like something out of *Hutchinson's*, but when the coppers pulled the masks off, who do you suppose was their ringleader?"

"A committee member named De Bow," Barham answered quietly.

Vale stared at him in consternation. "Bless you, Hawkshaw! Yes, Gideon De Bow, an unsuccessful painter who'd gotten himself in some financial straits and, knowing the club's schedule and having a key to the rear door, concocted a scheme for absconding with an armload of priceless treasures. The plan was to pile all the loot into some chest they have on display there and carry it away in one fell swoop. Now, before we get to the next lecture, tell me quickly, how'd you work out the solution?"

"It all revolved around the chest and the broken sword," Barham said. "Why was the chest standing open, when it was ordinarily kept closed? If the sword caused the scratches on its inside surface, as seemed likely, what were the circumstances? It occurred to me that the answer might be simple: the chest was open because someone had intended to place an item or items inside. But nothing had been taken from the room; in fact, from faint marks I noted in the dust, various items had instead been carefully returned to their places on the shelves. The most credible scenario was that Mr. Withrow had interrupted one or more thieves at their work and been struck down in a struggle, during which the damage to the chest had occurred, and at Mr. Mannering's noisy entry to the building the culprits had restored the room to its original state–though omitting, in their haste, to close the chest–and fled, fully intending to return at the next opportunity and carry out their planned theft."

"Jolly good. And as for the mastermind's identity?"

"The thieves must have fled through the rear door as Mr. Mannering entered from the front, meaning that they must have had a key to that door. They must also have been aware of the club schedule, that no one would have normally been around at ten o'clock or so on a Wednesday evening. As a member of the club committee, Mr. De Bow fit those criteria. Lastly, he gave himself away, when, upon the inspector's arrival in the depository, he referred to Mr. Withrow's being struck over the head. It was commonly understood that the steward had sustained his injury by striking his head against the floor; in fact, we had only learned otherwise shortly before that, at the hospital, and had not had occasion to mention the detail to anyone. The inspector of police had communicated only with the other Mr. Withrow at that point, so he could not have learned that fact from him. There was only one way De Bow could have known about the head wound."

The gaggle of students had reached the doors to the auditorium by then, and Vale shook his head with a grin as they stepped through the entryway. "You'd better be careful, old shoe. At the rate you're going, you'll find yourself saddled with a reputation before you know it–and not in the sciences!"

Though Torrington Square was no stranger to refined automobiles–the gentlemen staying in the residence hall there having, on the whole, any number of top-drawer connexions–the sample parked at the kerb that particular October evening was in a class by itself. A 1919 Hispano-Suiza H6 in a shade of blue so deep it was practically black, with a chauffeur in livery that was correct in every point, it awaited one specific scholar. The passenger in the rear of the phaeton had telephoned the individual in question the previous night with a peculiar message:

"Is this Owen Barham? My name is Doctor Alefounder. You don't know me, but an acquaintance of mine has a quandary, a sensitive situation which he would appreciate being able to discuss with you. You've been mentioned in certain circles as having a rare perspicacity, and if you are available tomorrow at this time…"

The chauffeur stepped down now as a young man emerged from the front entrance and moved briskly to hold the near-side rear door open for him. Alefounder, a stocky man with a thin white moustache, extended his hand to the young man. The only portion of the newcomer which could be clearly seen beneath the layers of overcoat, scarf, and hat were pale blue eyes framed by round spectacles.

"Mr. Barham? Welcome. Make yourself comfortable, or as comfortable as the evening air will allow. Our journey will not take long."

True to his words, the vehicle rumbled into life and sped swiftly past the British Museum and Piccadilly Circus, around Belgravia and past Hyde Park, and shortly drew up before a stately home in Kensington, one of those comprising the long grey-brick-and-white-pillar terrace on the north side of Onslow Square. The butler there swiftly divested Alefounder and his guest of their outer garments and murmured, "The master is awaiting you in the study. This way, please."

Blinking curiously at his surroundings, Owen Barham followed the others diligently and soon found himself in a pleasant yet dignified room, not particularly large, containing a smattering of books and writing implements and several comfortable-looking chairs arranged before a stone fireplace, in which a small fire was crackling. Before the fire stood a heavy but narrow-shouldered man, with a bristling walrus moustache and brooding deep-set eyes.

Alefounder said briskly: "Sir Galen, this is Owen Barham. Mr. Barham, this is Sir Galen Copper, the head of the Liberal Parliamentary Party."

Sir Galen took a final draw on the cigaret he was holding and threw it into the flames, turning with his large hand extended. "Thank you, Doctor. Have a seat, my boy. I imagine you're wondering why you were summoned here. You were recommended to me by a Mr. Arthur Snow of the Home Office, as having the acuity needed to grasp the solution to peculiarly opaque problems. I have a dilemma that I would be grateful to have you delve into, if you are willing."

While the doctor busied himself mixing drinks, Barham settled into one of the armchairs opposite the politician, as Sir Galen launched into his explanation.

"I don't know how conversant you are with the current political situation—you don't appear to be of voting age yet—but the Imperial Economic Conference began last week. Despite the name, the general tenor of the conference appears to be concerned with other topics effecting the Commonwealth. Nonetheless some of us have managed to put forward palpable warnings regarding the state of our nation's economy. The Battle of George Square, as it has come to be called, is a striking example that the lower classes will not forever tolerate these straitened conditions...

"On the week-end preceding the conference, I retired to my family's hunting lodge near Cheltenham to finish the speech I planned to give at the Conference–and to do a little hunting, of course. Certain key points in the speech were built around statistics in a report I had specially prepared for me by Martin Gillies-Glennie, Professor of Economics at the Royal College in Glasgow. You may imagine my great surprise, not to mention umbrage, at hearing, upon attending the Conference, the facts I had intended to hold forth on issuing from the lips of the Labour speaker. Understand me, if you will–it was not simply a matter of his orating on the same facts, it was a matter of his using a certain specific phrase from the report that had been sent to me. Here, these items will illustrate what I mean."

Sir Galen took up from the table at his elbow a page from a typed report, along with a newspaper folded to an interior column, and handed them across to Barham for comparison. Each was underlined in red ink at a certain point. The marked section of the report read:

"...As it stands the present state of affairs, as was said when I was a lad, is black as the Earl of Hell's waistcoat."

The newspaper read, in turn:

"...'The present state of affairs,' according to the Deputy Leader, 'is black as the Earl of Hell's waistcoat.' "

"There is no way on earth," Sir Galen growled, "that the double occurrence of an obscure Scottish simile is a coincidence. Somehow the Labour people got their hands on a copy of the report from Professor Gillies-Glennie. And it can't be that a set of prying eyes merely looked over the document; to echo the professor's words so closely I can only believe that a photographic record was made of the document and passed on to our worthy opponents.

"Your first question, no doubt, is whether the Labour speaker could have gotten a copy of the report directly from the professor. To that I respond that it is exceedingly unlikely they would have approached him for such a thing; there are economic savants at Oxford and Cambridge that they could have gotten in touch with far more easily. My own acquaintance with Gillies-Glennie is a personal one of long standing, and little-known outside my immediate circle. I might add that the professor's sense of honour is such that he would not give a duplicate report to a rival statesman, however tempting the inducement.

"Could the report, then, have been intercepted on its way to me? Impossible. It was placed directly in my hands by my secretary, Raleigh, just as I climbed aboard the train at Paddington Station. It was in a sealed envelope, fastened with the official stamp of the Royal College, and had not been tampered with, you may take my word on that. The report went into my case, where it remained for the duration of the journey west, and the case in turn remained within my reach, so there is no possibility of its being meddled with at any point during that time, either.

"It was not until the Saturday evening that I unsealed the envelope and placed the enclosed report on my writing desk, preparatory to beginning the final draft of my speech.

It remained on the desk, in plain view of anyone entering the study, until my departure for town on Monday morning. I had no concerns over that; all of my guests that week-end, with one exception, were members of my cabinet.

"Yet, at some point that week-end, one of these men, trusted senior members of the Party though they all are, entered my study and photographed the professor's report, later passing said photographs on to the opposition in Eccleston Square."

Sir Galen sighed. "The speech was a vexation–I hastily reworked my notes so as not to sound like a parrot when it was my turn at the lectern–but we'll fight on. I had two goals when attending this Conference, to bring attention to the economic issues that threaten to hobble our nation, and to reassure the voters of Clydeside, who have traditionally leant toward the Red end of the ballot, that we are aware of their situation and standing for them, by quoting a fellow Glaswegian's view of their plight. The first goal at least was realised, if not in the way I would have preferred, and we have hopes of carrying the Strathclyde district yet.

"What is weighing on my mind is the photographing of the professor's report. I would have sworn, before that week-end holiday, that every one of the men in my cabinet was loyal, to the Party and to me. But to know that one of them fed information to the Labour leaders, under the guise of accepting my hospitality, and has perhaps even been acting as an informer for some time...

"That, my boy, is the crux of the problem. How was it done? Not one of those men knew the report was in my possession, and so none of them could have come prepared to take photographs of it. Besides that, when would they have had the opportunity to do so? Between shooting, and cards, and billiards, not one of us was out of the others' sight long enough to manipulate a camera.

"What do you think, lad? Would you be willing to go further into this matter for me? I can arrange meetings with each of the men who were present at the hunting lodge, if you need, and with my head gamekeeper and the staff there. I even have–providentially–a photograph of my assembled guests, for your perusal."

Owen Barham had sunk into his armchair with his legs outstretched toward the fire, crossing them at the ankles, and during Sir Galen's recitation he had fallen into his usual trick of staring at his shoe-tips. Now he raised his head sharply, his eyebrows lifted in surprise above his spectacles, as the politician held out to him the photograph. It depicted a group of seven men in hunting tweeds, standing before a fireplace of rough-hewn stone in a wood-panelled room.

"Here, of course, am I, with my head gamekeeper, Budge. Proceeding to the left there are Evelyn Kenneworth; the Honorable Silas Martingale; Lieutenant Herbert Woodliff; Algernon Colfleet; and a friend of Colfleet's, a James Hughbanks. Hughbanks is the man who took the photograph; if you look closely you can make out the squeeze-bulb in his hand. Certainly I don't expect you to remember all these names, but I trust this demonstrates to you how willing I am to give you any and all information you might need in order to make some sense of this puzzle..."

"So there was at least one camera in use that weekend?" Barham asked. "I had the impression, from the way you spoke, that there was no indication that any of your guests had brought photographic equipment with them. But clearly one did."

Sir Galen waved one hand dismissively. "Hughbanks can be ignored. Every objection I've given you regarding the others applies more strongly to him. He isn't even a member of the Party. He'd have had no idea of the importance of the professor's report. He's an heir to a textile concern, and an amateur photographer on the side. We watched him unload his equipment from Colfleet's car, a great boxlike contraption with three spindly wooden legs, and cases for film and lightbulbs and who knows what else—and despite bringing all of that, it wasn't until the Sunday evening that he dragged it out and suggested a group portrait. It wasn't what you would call a roaring success. He got the camera in position, got us all arranged in front of the fireplace, and then discovered that there was a fault with one of his lenses, or bulbs, or some other piece of equipment. We were left standing about while he went to his room and got a replacement part from his baggage, for what felt like a quarter of an hour or more. But he did eventually get his photograph taken, as you see."

"Am I right in inferring that this group photograph was unexpected?"

"Exactly so. Originally it was to just be the five of us that week-end, and I had no notion of Hughbanks' coming until I saw him climb out of Colfleet's car. Never laid eyes on the man before then. Evidently he'd learned of our plans from Colfleet, who happens to be a neighbour of his, and cadged a last-minute invitation. Fortunately there are plenty of beds to be had at the lodge. First time the fellow'd ever been part of a hunting party, it seems, and after spending those days with him I'm not surprised. He could barely handle a firearm and was equally exasperating with a hand of cards or a billiards cue. Then, as I said, after a great deal of talk about his photographic hobby and how he had to take special care of his equipment, he forgot all about it until our final evening, and then herded us all together like a lot of schoolboys. Colfleet admitted to me at one point that he was sorry he'd let himself be talked into bringing the man."

"So there were to be four of your colleagues and you present at this hunting party. What about the staff at the lodge?"

"None of them had anything to do with this, I can assure you. As with Budge, who arranged everything for the week-end, they were all local lads. Barely able to read and write their own names, I shouldn't wonder; the importance of the professor's report would have been far beyond their grasp, and they had no time to fool about with a camera. No, the person responsible can only be one of a handful of men–and, at the very same time, cannot have been any of those men. A paradox!"

Owen Barham merely asked mildly, "What were the sleeping arrangements at your lodge? In other words, could someone have sneaked into the study during the night to photograph the report?"

"There is a connecting door between the master bedroom and the study, and I am a light sleeper. Similarly, Budge, who slept in a room at the end of the corridor–the beaters all went back to their own domiciles in the evenings–wakes easily. If anyone had been prowling about in the dark, one or both of us would soon have been aware of it."

"Have you considered the idea of an outsider entering the lodge while your group was out hunting? The report was in plain view on the writing desk, you said, easily gotten at by an intruder."

Sir Galen puffed out his heavy moustache. "One of the duties of a head gamekeeper is to be aware of what is happening on the estate at all times, to monitor the movements of those present so as to minimise the possibility of an unfortunate accident, given the discharging of multiple firearms in succession. You may be sure that Budge would have alerted me instantly had an automobile entered the grounds, or even an unexpected visitor on foot."

"Apart from Mr. Hughbanks, did any of the guests bring a noticeable amount of luggage with them?"

"No, just one or two cases apiece. We were only staying for the week-end, and there were no plans to dress for dinner or travel into town for any reason."

"You told me that you departed from Paddington Station–on that Friday evening, I assume. Did your other guests travel down to the lodge at the same time?"

"Kenneworth travelled on the same train as I. Martingale caught a later train. Colfleet–and Hughbanks, of course–and Lieutenant Woodliff drove down later."

"Did your train make any stops on the way? That is, could Mr. Kenneworth have had an opportunity to use the telephone before you arrived?"

Sir Galen stared at him quizzically. "Yes, there were several stops, and some of those stations no doubt have telephones, but Kenneworth never left our compartment. Nor did I."

Owen Barham nodded and handed the photograph back, and dropped his chin to stare once more at his shoe-tips. Sir Galen studied his visitor's face as the silence lengthened and finally cleared his throat.

"Have you any other questions for me? Or have you come to a conclusion? Will you be willing to inquire further into this matter? From what I've been told, if anyone can determine who might have known that the report was in my hands that week-end, you can."

Barham raised his head with a faint smile. "Actually, you yourself know of at least one person who had knowledge of the report, Sir Galen. Think back on the events you've described."

Dr. Alefounder, who had held his tongue until then, spoke in astonished tones. "Professor Gillies-Glennie? But you heard Sir Galen say–"

The politician cut off his friend's outburst with an irritated wave of his hand. Barham went on imperturbably.

"As a matter of fact, I was referring to your secretary, Mr. Raleigh. He knew that you would have the professor's report that week-end, since he placed it in your hands himself."

Sir Galen straightened up in his chair. "Raleigh? So you believe…"

"I have a hypothesis. More investigation would be needed to determine its validity. My suspicion is that your Mr. Raleigh is in the employ of the rival party and had instructions to pass on the information contained in the report as soon as he could. If the report had been delivered to your household earlier, he might have been able to copy it at his leisure, without your ever being aware of it. As it was, it arrived at the last moment, and he, knowing you desired to have it during your sojourn in the country, rushed it to the train station without being able to examine it.

"Mr. Raleigh then either contacted his other employer or contacted his fellow agent directly, to inform him that you were in possession of the professor's report. That other agent, Mr. Hughbanks–who I imagine has been cultivating an acquaintance with your Mr. Colfleet for some time–presumed on that acquaintance to get himself invited along on your week-end gathering, where he could take photographs of the report."

Sir Galen lifted one wide hand. "Hold, my boy. We aren't out of the woods yet. You tell me that Hughbanks was the one who took the photographs, but how is that possible? He was never apart from the others except on one occasion, when he had us pose as a group, and he left his camera behind with us, planted in the middle of the floor, while he went off to tinker with his equipment."

"Cameras come in all sizes, Sir Galen. Some–I'm thinking of the Kodak Brownie as an example–are small enough to slip into one's pocket. My supposition is that Mr. Hughbanks intentionally drew your attention to his full-size camera, referring to it multiple times in conversation and then manoeuvring the rest of you into a situation where you were left with the camera in plain view while he stepped out of the room, to preclude you from suspecting that he might have a second, smaller camera to hand.

"However, I say again, that is merely a hypothesis. What you will want are facts. I do happen to know of a private enquiry agent who might be willing to take up the matter, but I imagine you already have men at your disposal for such purposes."

"Quite so." Sir Galen gripped the arms of his chair determinedly, then rose to his feet with the distinctive motion that was well-known in the chambers of Parliament. "My boy, you have taken a great load off my mind tonight. I thank you for your time. It will be a pity to have to dismiss Raleigh, but halfway tolerable secretaries are ten a penny. I am much heartened to know that the integrity of the inner circle of the Party is intact, and the intelligence about Hughbanks and his spying for the opposition will be useful to us. I think we shall let him continue to believe that he is succeeding…"

Doctor Alefounder tapped Owen Barham on the shoulder, indicating with a gesture that it was time to depart. The great politician had turned toward the fire by then, taking out his silver cigaret case (something he had not extended to either of them at any point), and was speaking more to himself than to his guests. They left him there, as they slipped into their overcoats and stepped out into the chill silence of Onslow Square, staring up at the framed picture of Gladstone above his fireplace and weaving plans full of subtle yet artful machinations.

# The Deity of Durian

On that raw November day, in that particular stretch of bleak Suffolk coast, as in an artist's composition, one colour held mastery. The sky was burdened with isabelline clouds, rank upon rank of them; the waste ground that slanted imperceptibly from the main road down to the sea was dotted with clumps of sallow brush, shocked stiff beneath the north wind; and the line of low (very low) hills to the west of the road was mantled with vegetation in the same shade, obscured here and there by leafless dun-yellow trees and shrubbery of old brass.

This yellow motif was echoed in the two young men who made their way steadily up the road, with the collars of their overcoats turned up and scarves wound thickly about their throats. The taller of the two, broad in the shoulders and chest, had hair that bristled up, bright as butter, on his ruddy head and eyes that mirrored the dark blue-green of the North Sea depths. The other youth was pale and studious and slender, with hair as light as corn silk and water-blue eyes that looked out from behind round spectacles.

The larger boy was a local lad, Oxendine by name, and he had invited his companion, a fellow student of his at University College in London, to his family home in the village of Slaughden for the week-end, to experience the local festivities. His friend, Owen Barham, was a child of the East End, and had never seen a celebration as grand and boisterous as this one was to be–or so Oxendine proclaimed.

It was, in point of fact, Guy Fawkes Day, which fell on a Saturday in that year of 192-, but it was to be remembered long afterward in those parts for events quite distinct from the great bonfire and effigy-burning.

To pass the hours until the evening, Oxendine's suggestion was that they step out and take in the sights. They had been south of the village to the Martello tower; they had been along the quay to view the fishing boats, large and small; and now they were headed for the next town to the north. On its far side was a broad half-timbered Tudor building known as Moot Hall, which was used for events of any and all importance in the district, from weddings to elections, and on that day was to be the site of a public debate. A representative of a radical society was to argue with a local churchman regarding the effect on civilization of organised religion, and, to judge from the general state of affairs, whether there was even such a thing as a Supreme Being.

"They call themselves the Durian Society," Oxendine said by way of explanation. "The name is taken from an East Indian fruit that's said to be quite unpleasant in smell and taste, except to those who've grown accustomed to it, and to those initiated few it's delicious. That's their idea of a metaphor, don't you see–that truth, like the durian, is unpalatable to the great majority.

"Their leader is a chap called Cormac Conal O'Donoghue. He's one of those Irishmen who are the more dead-set against religion for having been steeped in it all their lives. He comes across as bold and acid-tongued, from the newspaper accounts, and is said to have lost very few debates against his more orthodox opponents. I'm looking forward to seeing what he'll do with the local divine.

"This parson, Abraham Monnett, is the leader of a small Nonconformist church in the area. I remember him vaguely from my boyhood, a wizened and grey-haired figure even then. I shouldn't wonder if they'll have to help him up onto the platform."

The auditorium, when they reached it, was already packed with spectators, but they managed to squeeze onto one of the benches in the back center of the room. The debate, fiery though it was, was inevitable in outcome almost from the start. The Reverend Monnett, his white hairs standing up stiffly at the back of his bald pate and curling up under his bony jawline, clutched rigidly at his lectern and failed utterly to make much of an impression on the crowd. O'Donoghue, on the other hand, cut a vividly theatrical figure. Clad in a light-coloured suit despite the season and with his dark hair sweeping in waves from his forehead, he paced back and forth with broad strides and gestures and punctuated his arguments by thumping the metal tip of his rattan walking stick on the platform. His Gaelic brogue, by turns sardonic and patronising, rang through the auditorium and overmastered the cleric's reedy tones. He began by acidly deriding the Church's efforts to help the poor and downtrodden by colluding with the blue bloods and the bankers, then moved on to depicting the Almighty as a trumped-up bogeyman meant to keep the working classes in their place, and finished by proclaiming that in this modern scientific age, no one of rational mind could believe in some mysterious divinity in the sky, when the very processes that generated life itself were being explicated day by day.

The result of the debate was mixed. The greater part of the crowd, comprised primarily of residents of the district, tended to agree with the Irishman's perspective on the monied estates and business owners, but were not quite ready to forswear their religious rituals and traditions. The rest, outsiders who had come primarily to witness their great paragon in action, were equally vocal in their views.

As they passed out with the clamorous throng, Oxendine and Barham could hear, above all of it, O'Donoghue's voice raised in vigorous discussion. Looking down the length of the building as they reached its corner, they saw the two debaters, their aides, and some local officials in a knot at the back of the hall. The tip of O'Donoghue's cane swirled in the air to underline some point, and as they looked on he swung on his heel and pushed through the ring of collocutors.

The young men turned their steps back toward the village of Slaughden, discussing the debate as they went, and like the crowd, their opinions were divided. Oxendine was firmly in O'Donoghue's camp, though not perhaps as far left-leaning in his political ideals.

"He's entirely correct, you know. Through the centuries the churches have encouraged the people to simply accept their political and monetary situation as God-ordained, depriving them of any reason to agitate for improvement. And has there ever been proof of an Eternal Deity, apart from some ancient writings of a nomadic Middle Eastern tribe?"

Owen Barham said quietly, "I don't know that the debate proved anything one way or the other. It seems to me that each side depends upon faith, loath as some are to admit it. When it comes to the beginning of the universe, either we accept the existence of a Creator whom no man has seen or ever can see, or we accept that inanimate matter somehow began combining into all the myriad forms we witness entirely by happenstance, and without any driving intellect behind it whatsoever."

"How else can it be? The natural laws are well-understood, thanks to Newton and Cavendish and those who've followed after them…"

The discussion had by no means ended by the time they reached Oxendine's home village and entered the inn, with the great whalebone hanging over its door. They leaned their elbows on the bar and ordered two pints of ale, and were signalling for a second round when the inn doors burst open and a youth flung himself inside with news.

"Murder! There's been murder done!"

They twisted around to stare at the interloper as the innkeeper said: "Will Crannis! What're you on about, lad?"

"They've found a dead man, at St. Audrey's well," said the boy. "That's one of them debaters, from up Moot Hall earlier. He was struck over the head, and a-layin' half in the water."

"One of the debaters?" asked Barham. "Which of them? Reverend Monnett, or Cormac O'Donoghue?"

"Is that the Irishman? No, 'twasn't him, but one of his lot. Some other man."

Oxendine looked at his friend eagerly. "Shall we go and see what's transpired?"

Barham demurred. "It's hardly any of my business…"

Oxendine snorted. "It's any man's business that can lend a hand. And we've no police in these parts except for a single constable; they'll have to send to Ipswich, to the

County Constabulary, for an inspector. In the meantime you've the most experience of anyone here at this sort of thing. Don't tarry, now!"

They hastened along with the boy Will to the next village, and beyond it, to a spot about a quarter-mile north of Moot Hall. A group of men were gathered at the road's edge with grim expressions. Among them were Cormac O'Donoghue and his disputative opponent; a short, stocky man in dark clothing holding a black doctor's bag; and a lanky figure in a dark-blue police uniform, with a bushy reddish-brown moustache too large for his face.

This latter individual turned toward the newcomers with the obvious intent of moving them along from the scene, but upon hearing Oxendine's description of his friend, and his deductive efforts in behalf of government officials and heads of state, the man pushed his constable's helmet back and scratched at his hairline.

"I'm to guard this spot 'til Inspector Worden arrives with his men," he muttered, "but if he's qualified as you say I don't s'pose it'll hurt to have the young gentleman look over the scene. Doctor Barlow?"

The doctor separated himself from the group and joined them. Alongside that section of road ran a small hill, shaped rather like a long barrow, and at its near end was a shallow cave, open on two sides. The constable–Cuffle was his name–led the four of them up a sloping footpath to the mouth of the cave, gesturing firmly for the boy to remain behind.

They bent down to look inside. For a moment it was if they had been turned entirely upon their heads, and the body within was about to slip forward and fall up, in Wonderland style, into a circle of yellowish-grey sky. It was a trick of perspective, of course: over the aeons a part of the limestone roof had eroded, leaving a sort of natural skylight above the pool at the back at the cave and making an empyrean mirror of the water's surface. The body, that of a man in his thirties, lay curled on its left side with its crown touching the ring of rocks around the pool.

"Talbot Puntney," said Cuffle. "You know the Puntneys, don't you, Oxendine?"

"Not well. He and his brothers were several years older than me, and already working when I was still in the schoolroom."

"He was one of the Durian Society people," put in the doctor. "The Puntneys are vaguely Church of England, and poor as Church of England mice, which perhaps explains how he came to fall in with that O'Donoghue and his crowd, with all their talk of guillotining the landlords and money lenders. He worked his way up to second behind O'Donoghue himself, though lately it seems he'd swung back in the other direction."

Owen Barham looked at him blankly, and Barlow explained with a gesture.

"This is a Marian well. Legend says that St. Audrey was fleeing from Framlingham Castle with two nuns, heading along the coast instead of directly west to her home on the Isle of Ely, in order to confuse their pursuers, when they stopped to slake their thirst at this well. Audrey was granted a vision of the Blessed Virgin as she drank, encouraging her to hold the faith. It's become a popular spot, particularly with the local women, to entrust their hopes to Audrey and seek cures for minor ailments–all the more so since the cave ceiling is low enough that most men can't step inside without stooping. I take Puntney's presence here as a sign that he'd reconsidered the existence of the Mother of God and her illustrious offspring."

"How was he killed?"

"He was struck at the base of his skull, while kneeling in prayer, I imagine. He'd fallen forward, with his face in the pool, and we had to drag him out to make an examination–something that it would be best not to circulate, I think. Spare the ladies' feelings, eh? The weapon was the proverbial blunt object, as far as I can tell. Something with a small, rounded edge–rather like a machinist's hammer, if I had to hazard a guess."

"But why on earth would a man of the cloth be carrying something like that around?" asked Cuffle.

"Not to mention that the lack of room in there wouldn't allow for a blow from above. The killer must have swung sideways–almost a forehand tennis swing–and can you imagine our dear doddering old cleric out on the court?"

"You have a definite suspect, then?" asked Barham.

Cuffle nodded. "Reverend Monnett was a-waitin' there by the path, about where he's standing now, when one of the people from Moot Hall come a-lookin' for Puntney, a clerk named Ffellowes. Mr. Monnett said he was a-waitin' for him, that he was in the cave, and when Ffellowes clumb up here to look he found Puntney dead. But apart from that there's no evidence; that'll be for Inspector Worden to discover. The murder weapon, whatever it might've been, is nowhere to be found. There's no scraps of cloth or loose threads in sight, and this ground's froze hard enough there's no chance of footprints in the cave or on the path."

"Could the method of the murder indicate special anatomical knowledge?"

"Possibly," said Dr. Barlow. "Or again it could have been entirely by chance. I don't know of too many men who are aware that the nape of the neck is a particularly vulnerable spot."

"Do you know of a motive for the crime?" Barham asked the constable.

"The details aren't entirely clear," Cuffle responded, "but it seems to've had something to do with a business venture, farming perhaps. There was some confrontation betwixt the three of 'em outside the Hall—"

"We heard some of it," said Oxendine wryly. "I imagine quite a few people did."

"Yers. Well, when Mr. O'Donoghue'd finished a-speakin' his mind, he stalked off and went a-walkin' up the road there to clear his head. We know at least he hasn't any part in this; he was seen to go and to return, by several folk, just as the body was a-bein' discovered."

Owen Barham looked over at the Irishman, who was standing with the group and yet apart from it. His only concession to the cold was a short cloak thrown about his shoulders, light both in colour and in weight, and a dark, wide-brimmed hat tilted rakishly across his curled head. He was leaning on his rattan stick with both hands and the knees of his trousers were faintly damp.

Barham asked mildly, "Does Mr. O'Donoghue give any explanation for the murder?"

"He says he reckons Reverend Monnett was angry about losing the debate and took his wrath out on the first Durian member he come across."

"And then stood waiting for the body to be discovered?" asked Oxendine.

Dr. Barlow nodded his acknowledgement of the point with a dry smile, while the constable shrugged in bafflement. Barham slipped his hands into his pockets.

He asked, "Is there anyone else who could tell us about the argument at Moot Hall?"

"That's the same fellow you want," said Cuffle, "this clerk named Ffellowes. He was with them as they come out of the Hall, and heard the meat of their conversation. He can tell you all about it. He's back there now, a-waitin' for his turn to be questioned and fixin' a room meanwhile for the inspector to use when he gets here."

"Would you mind if we spoke with him? I'd very much like to hear more about this."

"As you like. I'll be right here, if you happen to learn somethin' I ought to know."

When Barham and Oxendine reached Moot Hall, they found Ffellowes working in the auditorium with some other men, clearing away the benches from the floor. He was a slight man in his thirties, with wavy brown hair and a long, beaky nose. Despite having told his story to the constable, and knowing that he would soon be recounting it again to the inspector from Ipswich, he was perfectly willing to share it with the two young men–provided that they pitched in and helped move the remaining furniture.

"It's a shocking thing," he said, "this murder, but I'm not half surprised it happened. I suspected holding that debate here in the Hall was a poor idea, and there you are. Strong feelings on both sides, leading to a thing like this. And the irony is, the location was young Puntney's choice."

"It did occur to me," murmured Owen Barham, "that a little village by the sea was an unlikely backdrop for a man like Cormac O'Donoghue. It strikes me that he would have preferred a grander setting, one that would have guaranteed him greater publicity. Was the Hall chosen because Mr. Puntney was from this district?"

"That I couldn't say. All I know is that he suggested it to Reverend Monnett first, and then both of them reached out to us here at the Hall to arrange the details."

"I understand you were present after the debate, and witnessed the exchange that took place between the Reverend Monnett and the others?"

"I did. Puntney and the parson were in front a little ways, so I didn't catch all of what they were saying, but I did hear Reverend Monnett tell him, 'You know what is said about the man that observes the wind and regards the clouds. No good harvest can be reaped by that man.' Just then O'Donoghue, who was coming along behind me, pressed past and raised his voice to the minister. 'Poaching from my herd, are you?' he said. 'In my home country they've been known to take a dim view of that–the end of a rope, as a matter of fact.' The other two started to reply to him, at the same time, but he only twirled his stick in the air and said, 'I've no patience for this, and no intention of listening to those who refuse to shake off the blinders of superstition. You can keep your shackles. Fresh air is what I require. And Puntney–that which you do, do quickly.' Then he went off to fetch his cloak and hat, and the others went their way. That was the last I knew of it, until we got the news of Puntney's being found struck down at St. Audrey's well."

Barham looked troubled when Ffellowes reached the end of his testimony. He turned to his friend Oxendine with a frown.

"Constable Cuffle needs to be warned not to let Mr. O'Donoghue leave the area before Inspector Worden can speak to him. Go and tell him so, will you? Quickly!"

Oxendine returned from his errand to find that his friend had climbed up onto the platform and was sitting on its edge, his legs dangling over the side, looking out over the now-barren room. He dropped into place beside Barham.

"I told the constable what you said, and he'll keep O'Donoghue within reach... Let's see if I follow your thinking. You believe the Irishman saw something, or knows something, that's key to the identity of the murderer, don't you? Now what could it be...?"

"Oh, no," Barham said simply. "I believe he is the murderer."

Oxendine swung his head sharply to look at him. "What? How can you say that? You heard what Cuffle said. O'Donoghue went off up the road after that squabble outside the Hall and didn't return until after the body was found. More than one person can testify to seeing him."

Barham sighed. "Everyone seems to be forgetting that there is more than one way into the cave where Mr. Puntney was killed."

"Yes, it opens to the left and the right, but either way, someone climbing the path to the cave would have been noticed, if not by Ffellowes, by Reverend Monnett at the least. And I don't recall Cuffle referring even obliquely to that possibility."

"There's yet another way inside."

"You mean the opening in the roof above the pool? Surely you aren't suggesting that O'Donoghue squirmed into the cave through that hole?"

"Only in a manner of speaking. It would have been the easiest thing in the world for him to leave the road at any point he chose, climb to the crest of that small hill, and make his way back until he was standing directly above the cave. From that position he could take his opportunity, and strike the fatal blow."

Oxendine shook his head. "What about the murder weapon? Surely he's as unlikely as Reverend Monnett to have been carrying a machinist's hammer about with him."

"We saw the murder weapon ourselves. Every person in the audience today saw it, and watched Mr. O'Donoghue brandish it throughout the debate. His cane ends in a metal ferrule, and that rattan stick is an indispensable part of his costume. You remember how the doctor described the weapon–something with a small, rounded edge."

"And his motive?" Oxendine asked, with an air of bemusement. "What possible reason could he have had to murder one of his own adherents?"

"The key to the entire situation lies in that conversation outside the Hall, following the debate. Mr. Ffellowes altogether missed the significance of the remarks made by Reverend Monnett and Mr. O'Donoghue. The reverend's comments to Mr. Puntney were not in connexion with agriculture; they were an allusion to a passage in Ecclesiastes, a warning against allowing potential difficulties to dissuade one from taking action. Clearly, Puntney was considering some step which held the possibility of a thorny outcome. A Biblical reference is to be expected coming from the mouth of a clergyman, but O'Donoghue's rejoinder is even more striking. He first accused the reverend of poaching, then made a Scriptural quotation himself–this from a man who has no more regard for the Bible than for the *Morning Post*! His parting words were those Jesus uttered when dismissing Judas Iscariot–'That thou doest, do quickly,' in the version we know.

"Do you see the portrait painted by all that? Mr. O'Donoghue regards himself as a latter-day Jesus of Nazareth, gathering a group of loyal followers determined to tear down all that he views as defunct and pernicious to society–religious institutions, the nobility, banking and commercial enterprises. To learn that one whom he viewed as his right hand in this crusade was considering turning his back on it all and returning to the churchly fold–to his mind that was nothing more than rank betrayal. I suspect he had learned about Mr. Puntney's planned visit to the holy well in one way or another, and with this defection burning in his mind he turned back and approached the site from above, wishing to peer down at his former comrade as he prostrated himself in foolish devotion.

"Picture the scene. O'Donoghue, with his anger and wounded pride surging up in his breast, looks down through the opening in the rock and sees the back of Puntney's neck, exposed as he bends his head in prayer, exposed as if to the executioner's blade. O'Donoghue drops to his knees there at the edge of the opening, in a twisted reflection of the other man's pose–thus the damp spots on the knees of his trousers, from the frost-rimmed grass–and, raising his cane, thrusts it downward with all his might, to strike down his betrayer."

Owen Barham shook his head. "It's a dangerous thing, his sort of enterprise: this conviction that the only way for society to proceed is for men to attack and tear down all that previous generations have held sacred. After every god and idol have been brought low, their feet of clay smashed to pieces, the only god left may be the one in the mirror."

Human nature being what it is, it was inevitable that Owen Barham's friends and fellow students would not only view his deductive abilities as fascinating fodder for conversation but would come to treat them as a sort of legerdemain, to be called forth upon demand.

One cold and blustery evening toward the beginning of winter, at the end of a long day filled with long and enervating lectures, a group of weary scholars–Barham among them–returned briefly to their rooms to shed their academic robes like a flock of moulting crows and then trotted around to the Barleycorn, a favourite pub of University College students. As they downed their pints one of them called for an evening newspaper and began riffling through its pages with a gleaming eye.

"Here, Young Man in the Corner," he said at last. "Let's see you work your magic on this. What do you make of it?"

He folded the newspaper over and thrust it under Barham's nose, indicating with a square-tipped finger an article in the international section, with the headline "Trial To Proceed For Accused Expatriate."

> *French Riviera, today*– Examining Magistrate Etienne Dupâquier, speaking from the Palais de Justice in Nice, confirmed that his office will proceed with the case against Sylvester Ryecroft, who is accused of the murder of his uncle, Arthur Finucane. Readers will recall that Finucane, an Irish landowner and inventor, was found

dead in his villa in the Boulevard Soleau earlier this month.

Ryecroft continues to insist on his innocence of any involvement in the poisoning death of Finucane, carried out by oleander in his tea, but every indication points to his guilt. Not only had Ryecroft borrowed heavily from his uncle on multiple occasions and expected a large gain as one of his heirs; not only are oleander plants part of the décor at the Hotel Hermitage, where Ryecroft maintains a set of rooms; but a figure matching Ryecroft's description was seen turning down the Rue Bonaparte, near the crime scene, by a policeman on patrol, as well as by Finucane's manservant shortly before the murder occurred.

The strongest mark against Ryecroft, though, is the question of his alibi. While admitting that he was drinking heavily on the evening of the murder, he claims to have been on the telephone with his uncle's lawyer in Ireland from around 5.25 to 5.50. If true, this would have made it impossible for him to have arrived at his uncle's house a few minutes before 6.00 (the time noted by Finucane's manservant). Ryecroft does not own an automobile, and the time to walk to his uncle's villa would be at least twenty minutes, according to the official police reenactment. When questioned, however, the lawyer, one Mr. Mucklebreed, stated clearly that their conversation took place between 5.00 and 5.25, giving Ryecroft ample opportunity to reach his uncle's villa and commit the crime.

Ryecroft has engaged Maître Sabouraud, of the celebrated firm of Ardisson et Cabanel, for his defense.

Owen Barham reached the end of the article with his brow furrowed. He removed his round spectacles and polished them abstractedly with his handkerchief. His chums waited expectantly for some great pronouncement from him, but all he said was, "I'd like to know more about the case. Do you think we could get hold of some older newspapers, with more details?"

His friend Jimmy Clough replied, with a knowing smile, "You're on to something, aren't you?"

"I have an idea. Do you remember telling me about that farmer from Donegal?..."

The two of them rose from the table and approached the publican, a somewhat harassed-looking man with a weedy moustache and rolled sleeves, to ask if he had older newspapers on hand. Like many people, he indeed kept a stack of them in a back room, for use as scrap material after they had ceased to be of any other interest. He called for his daughter to show them where the papers were kept, and lifted the hatch briefly for the two young men to pass through into the back rooms.

The publican's daughter turned out to be a plump blonde with large, wide-spaced violet eyes. She and Barham did the greater share of the winnowing, while Clough tried to entertain her with a line of patter. In the end they emerged with two sheets of newsprint, which Barham spread out on the bar top.

The first was from two weeks prior, with a brief article titled "Arrest In Poisoning Case."

> *French Riviera, today–* Inspector Dauzat of the Nice police announced a development in the Arthur Finucane poisoning case. The deceased's nephew, Sylvester Ryecroft, was taken into custody late last evening, and questioning is ongoing.
>
> Ryecroft is a familiar figure in clubs and nightspots along the French coast. He is a member of the leisured class, existing on a modest legacy from his deceased parents, supplemented by periodic loans from his late uncle and occasional winnings at various racetracks and casinos. He is known for his distinctive costume, usually sporting a colourful ascot and a porkpie hat, and is well-known in his uncle's neighbourhood due to his frequent visits there.

> According to Inspector Dauzat, there can be little doubt that they have the correct person in hand. Without delving into specifics, he stated that Ryecroft appears to meet the three criteria sought by police under these circumstances: motive, means, and opportunity.

The second page was from a newspaper three days before that, and contained an article headed "Questionable Death Now Homicide Enquiry."

> *Nice, today–* French police have confirmed that the death of an Anglo-Irish resident is now being investigated as murder. Arthur Finucane, 62, was found dead in his villa in the Boulevard Soleau on the morning of the 7th, from what was originally assumed to be a heart attack. Further investigation and chemical analysis have determined that the cause of his demise was the presence of oleander in his tea, with two hastily-washed teacups among the evidence found at the scene.
>
> Indications are that death occurred the previous evening, while the deceased was playing a game of chess with a visitor. It appears this visitor then removed the teacups and dragged the body to a chair in the next room, placing an open book in Finucane's hand, in a

clumsy attempt to make it seem that the Irishman had passed away at a later time, and from natural causes.

Finucane's manservant, Honoré Beaud, was able to confirm that his master was expecting a visitor on the evening of the 6th, at 6.00. He himself did not see the visitor enter, being in the larder arranging items for the next day's menu, but he heard the person arrive at 5.56, according to his watch. Finucane himself admitted the guest to his study with the words, "Come in, my boy"– this seeming to indicate some measure of familiarity between the two of them. Beaud, having been granted the evening off, departed shortly afterward, and while he did not see the guest (the study door being closed by then), he was able to describe for the police certain distinctive garments he noticed hanging on the coatrack beside the front door.

Inspector Dauzat stated that their primary goal at this juncture is to locate the mysterious visitor. They have been in touch with the deceased's heirs for assistance, as well as his family lawyer in Ireland, and they urge anyone with information relevant to the crime to come forward.

Finucane was a semi-retired landowner and amateur inventor,

> having developed variations on the hip bath and the clock-phonograph, among other things. He divided his year between his ancestral estate in the village of Glentornan in western Ireland and his villa in Nice. He is succeeded by his son, Ronan Galbraith, a businessman well-known in the brokerage houses of the Old Town, and a nephew, Sylvester Ryecroft, who is of independent means.

"I wonder," Barham said. "Do you suppose there's an atlas anywhere near at hand?"

They applied once more to the publican, who, his hands full dispensing drinks to a room full of noisy students, waved a hand irritably in the direction of his daughter. She disappeared into the back rooms and shortly brought forth a wide volume, which the two young men opened with alacrity. Clough stabbed his finger at the map of Ireland with relish.

"There it is, sure enough. Right in the heart of County Donegal, just a stone's throw from Donegal Town."

"There's a distinct possibility, then... What we need is a token for the telephone–and possibly more than one."

Tokens in hand, the pair moved over to the public telephone, mounted on a board on the wall as in many such establishments, and Owen Barham launched into an explanation with the operator involving his attempts to reach a lawyer in the vicinity of Donegal Town named Mucklebreed. No, he did not have a telephone number or an address or even a first name. Yes, he knew that it was after office hours; that was why he was trying to reach Mr. Mucklebreed at home.

When, after some effort, the situation was untangled and a connexion was finally made, the ring was answered by a female voice, young and adenoidal, speaking in pure Gaelic. Barham thrust the earpiece at his friend. It took several minutes for Clough to attain results, but when he finally replaced the earpiece on its cradle he was grinning as wide as could be.

"That was our Mr. Mucklebreed's maid," he said. "I had to exercise every bit of my charm on the poor confused colleen to get her to answer those few wee questions, but it's just as you thought. It even happens the lawyer lives in that very same village of Glentornan as his late client, right down the lane in fact. I convinced her in the end to tell me the time the clocks in the house are set to–and I made certain that he keeps his pocket watch set to the same time– and wouldn't you know it, it's 5.40 in that good man's home… They're a stubborn lot, those people of Donegal."

He flashed his black eyes significantly at the clock hanging behind the bar, courtesy of the Nine Elms Brewery. Barham followed his friend's gaze and nodded.

"Now I need to try to make another call… Do you know if anyone in our group speaks French?"

"At least one, for sure… Hoy! Ambleton! Come here, boyo!"

The individual thus addressed wended his long-boned frame through the crowd to the instrument hanging on the wall and the same routine was repeated, this time to the south of France.

Two days later the group of students was again gathered around a table in the Barleycorn, this time with a newspaper in the middle of the table bearing the headline "Reversal In Murder Case: Nephew Released, Son Arrested." The young man who had on the previous occasion picked out the newspaper article for Owen Barham to peruse sat back in his chair, his hand gripping his pint glass, and shook his head at the other.

"All right, we've each of us read the article. We know the details: how the inventor's son, having emptied his coffers due to rash speculation on the stock market and brought himself nearly to ruin, decided to hasten his inheritance with a pointed application of oleander from his back garden; how he decided to cover himself in case foul play was suspected by dressing in the ascot-and-porkpie-hat ensemble favoured by his dissolute cousin; and how the accused's attorney was able to solidify his client's alibi for the time of the murder in light of certain points made by 'an interested party in London.'

"Now will you tell us what the devil put you onto the right scent? And what on earth it all has to do with some farmer in Donegal?"

Owen Barham smiled slightly. "Six or seven years ago," he said, "the Irish government decided that it would be practical and beneficial to join its neighbours to the east, England and France, in following Greenwich Mean Time. Up to that point the country went by its own official time, set by Dublin.

"Not every citizen was keen on the change. One farmer, who lived in the area of Donegal, was interviewed by a newspaperman about the decision–this was the story Jimmy related to me–and his reply was that he had no intention of changing his clocks, no matter what the officials in Dublin did. 'I rise when the cows do,' he said, 'and I go to bed when they're abed. Tinkering with the clocks won't make any difference to them, and I can't see any bally sense in my doing it.'

"When I read about the 'phone call in the case, to the lawyer in Ireland, it recalled that story to my mind, and I wondered if there might possibly be something to it. The point, you see, is the difference in time between the two locales. The previous Irish time was exactly twenty-five minutes and some seconds earlier than Greenwich standard—and that's the time the village lawyer, Mucklebreed, is still following.

"The officials questioned each of them and got distinctly different answers. Ryecroft claimed that he placed his call from 5.25 to 5.50, leaving him unable to reach his uncle's house in time to commit the murder, while Mr. Mucklebreed claimed that the call was from 5.00 to 5.25—and they were both telling the truth! The whole thing hinged on one simple fact, which it never occurred to anyone to check. The investigators asked the lawyer for the time of the call—but they never thought to ask him what the time was there, at his house."

# The Galthorpe Gemini

The night can fall with appalling swiftness in the English countryside in winter, but Owen Barham and Thomas Silver had this advantage at least: the landscape in every direction was covered with a blanket of crystal that shone blue-white under the moonlight and silvery-gold where the beams of the Austin's headlamps touched it.

It was the middle of December, and they were driving back from Margate, where Silver had been employed to resolve a jewel theft at the Terrace Hotel. He had hoped to make it back to London before midnight, but the snow, which had fallen heavily all through the previous day and only tapered off that morning about two hours after sunrise, was proving a true adversary. Work crews had been out with wagons and shovels in an attempt to make the roadway passable, but the going was still much slower than usual, with the result that it was already past six o'clock and they were less than halfway through their journey. Wrapped up as thoroughly as Wells' famous Invisible Man against the cold air, hunched into their heavy overcoats and still half frozen through, not to mention distinctly puckish–it was little wonder that when Silver caught sight of a signpost reading "Galthorpe–2 mi" with a faint glow some distance beyond it, he swung the car off the main artery in the direction indicated.

The lesser road they found themselves on had not been touched by the work crews, but at least one vehicle had passed that way before them, so that Silver had a clear track to follow. Shortly, just around the second curve to the right, they came into the main street of the village, and with it the village inn, marked by a great sign bearing the legend

"The Old Sparrow Hawk"–and an equally great clutter of vehicles in front of it.

"Surely that's not usual," Silver muttered through his muffler. He rolled past the front door until he found a spot to squeeze the Austin into, and the two of them grabbed up their suitcases and plunged into the building.

Inside it was warmer than expected, and quite noisy. The bar was packed with men, in what appeared to be two general clusters, and the fireplace in the corner was blazing away. In the room beyond, the bar-parlour, more men were gathered.

The innkeeper came forward, a dark and hirsute man with rolled-up sleeves, and stared at them charily across the counter. "Can I help you gentlemen?"

"Is there any chance you have a room to spare?" asked Silver. "I see you've a good-sized crowd here…"

"You've come late to the pea-hucking," the man replied obscurely, "but as it is, I've one room left, a small one away in the back. I think you'll find it'll do. I'll have the girl take your bags up." He tapped the bell on the counter.

"And a meal?" Silver added quickly. "We're not particular, as long as the food is hot."

"Just step over into the dining room, across the passage, and I'll send her in shortly. You can hang your coats by the fire."

They did as bid, leaving their overcoats steaming away on pegs next to the fireplace. The dining room was dark-panelled, as were the other rooms, and they had it all to themselves. "The girl," presumably the innkeeper's daughter or niece, came in after nearly an hour, with a tray bearing pints of ale and plates of food. She was a sturdy damsel with ash-blond hair tied back in two braids, and a knowing expression on her broad face.

"You're reporters too, are you?" she asked as she placed the plates in front of them.

"Only a pair of travellers," Silver said. "I take it something newsworthy has happened hereabouts?"

"Oh, yes. Murder, and a manhunt too. Be the talk of the whole country by tomorrow, I don't doubt. The bar's full of them newspapermen, just a-waitin' to get the whole story, and the parlour's full of policemen down from Maidenstone. You're sure you don't know nothing about it?"

"Not a solitary thing."

The girl's eyes took on a gleam at this newfound outlet for her knowledge. Her listeners tucked into their food like trenchermen as she rattled off the details. Their plates held thin strips of beef, mashed potato with shallots, and some other root vegetable, possibly swede or turnip, boiled in a watery sauce. It was, as Silver had expected, not particularly flavourful but certainly piping, and a welcome feeling of warmth began to pervade them.

"The miller's wife was killed by his brother, and her jewels took. He run out of their cottage and disappeared completely. They've searched every house in the village for him, and the police are a-workin' out what to do next.

"When I say the miller's wife, I mean to say she was the new miller's wife, but then she was the old miller's wife too–what I mean is, she was the widow of the old miller, Tobias Priest. He died from a fall off his tower near a year ago now. Then, six months ago, this Spanish fellow come to town a-lookin' to take over the miller's place, and took up courting her, too. His name was Carlos Laza. They was wed soon after and started up the mill again.

"Then, a week ago, the miller's brother Rafael come to live with them. His twin brother, that is—looked the spitting image, he did, excepting he had a pirate's moustache and a patch over his eye. Pure sour-looking, he was. And a surly sort—didn't hardly speak no English, and had some peculiar habits too.

"I s'pose we shouldn't none of us been surprised at his a-goin' and doing a thing like this, after all. Mrs. Laza—it's hard not to call her Mrs. Priest still—said the brother wouldn't talk to her and wouldn't take meals with them either. Took all his meals in his room, carried up by Mr. Carlos on a tray. She said they two talked together regular-like on those occasions, with no shouting or carrying on, but the brother just wouldn't spend time with them.

"Then, this morning, about nine o'clock, just after the snow'd stopped coming down, Mr. Carlos come a-runnin' into town, a-cryin' that his wife had been killed. He said Mr. Rafael'd come this way, that he'd followed his footsteps in the snow but lost him. Put the whole village in an uproar."

"He lost his brother's trail, you say?"

Silver put the question out of politeness more than anything else. As a private enquiry agent he had occasionally delved into matters of murder—but only when commissioned to do so. At the moment he was more interested in mundane topics like food and rest. The girl took a breath to launch into explanation when the innkeeper called sharply to her.

"Maud! Stop a-dawdlin', girl, them gentlemen don't want to be bothered by the likes of you!"

"Mr. Rafael's footprints come straight to the edge of the village and then vanished completely!" she gushed. "But if you want to know the details, you'd best ask Mr. Adder, the baker's assistant. He was the one heard the whole story. That's him in there, the short one with the sandy hair. He can tell you all about it."

She bustled away, and Silver looked across at his companion with a humourous glint. The bespectacled young man sitting opposite him was a university student, with even less cause than he to become involved in criminal investigation, but Owen Barham had nonetheless developed a reputation for becoming entangled with odd and unusual puzzles.

"Vanishing footprints," he murmured. "You want to hear more about that, don't you?"

"As long as we're here..." Barham returned with a smile.

They carried their pint glasses into the bar. The man Maud had indicated sat at a large table in the center of the room, apparently one of a group of locals. He was indeed on the short side, stocky and pug-nosed, with a thatch of straight sandy-brown hair drooping across his forehead.

"Mr. Adder?" asked Silver.

The man lifted his head with a frown. "Tom Adder— that's me. More reporters, is it? Don't you think you'd be more comfortable with your friends back there?" he asked, hooking his thumb over his shoulder.

Silver glanced briefly at the reporters gathered around the corner tables, buzzing like flies, with one or another occasionally making for the telephone hanging in the passageway, and shook his own head.

"We aren't newsmen, just interested parties. I understand that you know the most about what's happened. If you wouldn't mind telling the story once more, we'd be glad to listen. And I think you'll agree a fresh round wouldn't be out of order..."

With full pint glasses in front of him and his friends Adder's attitude thawed somewhat. He leaned forward on his thick forearms as the other men made room for Barham and Silver to pull chairs up to the table.

"It was this morning, about nine o'clock, that it all come out," Adder began. "The snow'd stopped coming down shortly before that, but we was out even before it did, a-workin' to clear the street so folks could get out and about. Knee-deep, it was. There was two crews of us, a-workin' from each end of the high street, to get it clear first afore moving out from there. I was in charge of the crew a-workin' from the east, the butcher had charge of the crew on the west part of the village.

"The high street runs east to west. We'd just worked our way up to the point where it meets Tower Street. That's the street runs north out of the village to the sea, past the mill. As we come to Tower Street I happened to look in that direction and saw Carlos Laza coming, a-callin' out and a-wavin' his arms. Mr. Laza, he's the miller for the district.

"I could see it all clear as diamond as I come close to him, the whole world covered with white from end to end, the miller's cottage and the windmill white as well, with a faint grey stripe of sea beyond. The only bit of colour in all of it was the red tiles on the cottage's roof and the top of the tower, but even them was capped with snow. Believe me, there wasn't a thing moving in all that landscape, not a soul to be seen nowheres—and you'll see why I tell you that, in a moment.

"Now you should know about Mr. Laza, and them living there at the mill. Mr. Laza was from Spain originally I take it, just whereabouts I'm not sure, but he come here from Faversham. We'd lost our old miller, Mr. Priest, in an accident about a year ago, and the news that we was without a working mill had spread all along this stretch of coast. It was six months ago he arrived to take up the position, and to have Mrs. Priest's hand in marriage as well. Betwixt the two of them they got the mill up and running again. Then, two weeks ago, Mr. Laza got a letter from Faversham saying his brother was on the way here, to stay with them.

"The brother, Rafael Laza, arrived in town last week. Turned out he and Mr. Carlos was twins, alike as peas in a pod—up to a point. The brother was an unsociable sort—could be he didn't speak more than a few words of English—and had a patch over his left eye and a great bandit's moustache. He didn't take to his brother's wife any more than he did to the rest of us, wouldn't be in the same room as her if he could avoid it. Mr. Carlos had to resort to carrying his brother's meals up to his room on a tray."

Silver had lit the long clay pipe which he favored, and interjected, "How were relations between the brothers?"

"That I couldn't say. But I never saw the two of them together, if that tells you anything, and nor did anyone else."

"Carlos Laza didn't introduce his brother to the townspeople?"

"No, first we knew Rafael Laza was here was when he come into town to make some purchases."

"Anything unusual?"

"Nothing to indicate he was planning a murder," Adder said wryly. "No, he bought some hair lotion and a carton of cigarettes the first time he was in town, a couple loaves of bread the second time. That was all anyone saw of him, just them two occasions.

"Then, this morning, here come Carlos Laza a-callin' out bloody murder. 'Have you seen him?' he says. 'Have you seen my brother? He's killed my wife!' "

"Wait until you hear this next part," added a dark-haired man with a heavy pipe, who was sitting on Owen Barham's left.

Adder proceeded: "He pointed to a set of tracks in the snow, aside his own. I could see them clear. They come from the mill and headed into town, and then, just about a stone's throw from the furthest cottage out, the widow Lambe's place, they stopped completely. Come to a full dead end.

"He told me he'd found his wife dead in her bed, strangled, her jewelry box empty, and his brother gone. He'd followed his brother's tracks out of the cottage and down the road to the village–but where did Rafael Laza go from there? That's the grand question. Where could he've gone in all that snow-covered landscape without leaving any footprints behind? I promise you, there wasn't none, in any direction. They just come to a stop there in the middle of the road."

"Such things aren't unheard of, of course," said the man with the heavy pipe. "There was a case in the States about forty years ago, in a place called South Bend, very similar to this one. A young boy went outside to his family's well on Christmas Eve and disappeared completely. The only trace he left behind was his footprints in the snow—and those stopped halfway to the well."

"Was he ever found?" asked Barham.

"Never seen alive again."

"Yes, you've told us all about it, Relish. This is Eugene Relish, our chemist," Adder added in explanation. "Well, at hearing Laza's story, I went for the village constable. That sort of thing is his business. He collected the doctor and we trooped up to the miller's cottage. Found it just as he said, his wife lying dead in bed, the jewelry box emptied, and the room where the brother was staying empty as well, with the bureau drawers left half pulled-out. Not that Mrs. Laza had much in the way of jewels, just a few old pieces she'd inherited and a necklace her first husband had bought her—it's not a wealthy life, being the wife of a miller—but every last piece was gone."

"At least Laza won't do too badly for himself," put in Relish. "There is that life insurance, after all."

Silver and Barham looked inquiringly at him, and the chemist said, "I didn't hear this firsthand, mind you, that isn't how news spreads in a small village, but it seems Carlos Laza purchased life insurance for the pair of them a few months after they were married. He told his wife that he'd been thinking about the way her first husband had passed, dying in an accident like he did, and that something like that could happen to one of them, and they ought to have some provision if it did. I believe the policy is worth around £500 or so."

"After Hake, our constable, examined the scene," Adder said, "he herded us all out of there and called for the men from the County Constabulary. They sent out an inspector from Maidenstone, Ainsworthy by name, and he and his men are in the parlour there now, a-plannin' their next move."

"So it was a robbery, and nothing else?" asked Silver.

"What else could it be? Rafael Laza, much as he avoided her, hadn't any reason to want his sister-in-law dead, other than to take her jewels."

"Was the victim an invalid, or bed-ridden when she died?" asked Owen Barham.

The men stared at him. Silver, who had learnt from experience that the odder and more disconnected his young friend's questions appeared, the more significant they were, sat back with a smile playing upon his lips.

"Hardly," replied Adder. "Bitsy Laza was strong as a horse, and wasn't sick barely a day in her life. She certainly wasn't ailing when she died."

"But she was killed in her bedclothes?"

"That's right. Rafael Laza must've struck her down early in the morning, afore the snow'd stopped a-fallin', and fled from their cottage right after. His footprints wasn't half as clear as his brother's coming after him."

"Did the first set of footprints seem unusual in any way?"

"They was less clear, as I say, with the snow coming down atop them... and seemed a bit irregular-shaped, I s'pose being made in the heat of the crime and all."

At that moment the village constable emerged from the bar-parlour, heading for the counter for a pint, and Adder called to him.

"Hake! Bring your glass over here. We've a young man here has some questions about our murder–and no, he's not another newsman."

The constable approached. He was rather pear-shaped, with a round head at the end of a long neck and a body that sloped downward from small shoulders to a thick waist. The hair that covered his scalp and made up his toothbrush moustache was almost as pale as Owen Barham's own. He held himself with the stiff-backed dignity common to village policemen, and looked severely down at the ring of men around the table.

"I can't be a-talkin' to just anyone about an ongoing investigation…"

Adder wagged his head. "Don't play the grand copper with us, Hake. Just answer the lad's questions."

Barham asked, "Is it true Mrs. Laza was still in her bedclothes when she was killed?"

"That's right," Hake said. "Suffocated with one of her pillows sometime during the morning."

"I've been told she was in good health when she died. Do you know if she was an early riser, or habitually slept late?"

"Wouldn't have been much use as a miller's wife if she stayed abed all morning," said Adder. "We country folk can't be a-wastin' daylight. Too much to be done."

"Even in the winter?"

Constable Hake said slowly, "It's true, the mill don't generally operate in the winter, but there's still tasks to be done around the place. Gears to be kept greased, the sails to be checked over for ice, the stones to be dressed–though that last's not done every year. Bitsy Laza'd have been up first thing every morning, to get her husband's tea a-brewin' and breakfast ready."

"Was there a kettle of tea on in the kitchen?"

Hake stared at the young man. "Can't say, I'm sure. You reckon all these details of their domestic arrangements are important somehow?"

"I think the facts ought to be correlated as far as possible. Did the victim and her husband sleep in the same bed?"

"They did."

Barham continued, with his brow furrowed: "Were her jewels the only things taken? Nothing else was missing from the cottage?"

"Mr. Laza says not. The jewelry box was on a chest of drawers beside the bed, and was open and empty when we looked over the scene."

"Did you see the room where Rafael Laza was supposed to be staying?"

"Of course. The drawers in that room was pulled open and empty too, and the bedsheets ruffled. Whatever trunk or valise he'd brought with him was gone, took when he fled."

"Is it certain that no one ever saw the two brothers together, and that Rafael Laza avoided being seen by the victim?"

"That's what Mrs. Laza told Mrs. Greaves and Mrs. Olive, among others. She heard him a-movin' around in his room at times, heard her husband and him a-talkin', but he wouldn't show his face when she was around... As far as the two brothers, it's true enough, they didn't come into the village together. Rafael Laza come into town on just two occasions, to make some purchases, and his brother wasn't with him. But there couldn't be any doubt in anyone's mind they was brothers, and twin brothers at that. You can ask the postmaster, the baker, Mr. Relish here–anyone who saw him. The two of them was two sides of the same coin, except for Rafael's moustache and eye patch."

"Tell me about the footprints in the lane. The ones made by Rafael Laza ended short of the first cottage on that side of the village, where a certain widow lives. How is that woman's eyesight?"

"Georgetta Lambe?" asked Adder. "Can't see barely past the end of her arm, the old crow."

Barham asked the constable, "Did anything about those prints strike you or the inspector as strange, especially when compared with Carlos Laza's footprints?"

Hake looked at the young man quizzically. "Rafael Laza's prints was… smudged, you might say. 'Course they'd been made when the snow was still coming down, while his brother's was made afterward, and fresh and sharp."

"Were there any other footprints around the miller's cottage, or any unusual marks inside or outside?"

"The ground around it was completely unmarked–except for a set of tracks out to their well and back, that is. No doubt one of them a-goin' out to draw some water for the morning's tea."

Owen Barham fell silent, and Silver, recognising the abstracted expression on his friend's face, said, "You have an explanation, don't you?"

"I have a hypothesis," Barham began fastidiously, using a phrase his acquaintants had come to know well, but he was interrupted by the chemist, jabbing the air with the short stem of his pipe.

"An explanation? You mean you, a stranger here, after a single conversation with us, have an answer to this mystery? You can explain how a man can disappear from an empty country lane without leaving a single trace behind him?"

It was Barham's turn to speak slowly, as if still mulling over the idea that had occurred to him.

"What if he didn't? What if, in fact, Rafael Laza never existed at all?"

If the locals had stared at the bespectacled young Londoner before, they were absolutely staggered now. The reporters clustered in the corner, who had been half-listening to the conversation in the off chance that some new fact might come to light, had stopped their buzzing, and were craning their necks forward to catch Barham's words.

"Never existed?" exploded Adder. "Why, lad, we've told you how many people in the village saw him–on two different occasions!"

"He was seen, yes," Barham replied. "But he was never seen when Carlos Laza was present, by any villager, and apparently not by Mrs. Laza either. And think by how simple an alteration the one could be made to look like the other–a false moustache and an eye patch, nothing more."

"So you're saying..." prompted Hake.

"The circumstances of the murder, as described, simply don't make sense. Mrs. Laza was killed in her bedclothes, and she had no known reason for lingering in bed, so she must have been killed early in the morning, before she would normally have risen. Why? Either Carlos Laza was such a sound sleeper that he could lie insensate while his wife was in her death throes mere inches away–incredible, but not impossible–or he was involved. Only the second explanation seems plausible. If robbery had been the true motive, and there is in fact much to be done at the windmill even in winter, then it would have been far easier to wait until Mr. and Mrs. Laza were occupied elsewhere and their bedroom unattended.

"I propose that the theft of the jewels was nothing more than an attempt to put forward a believable motive for the murder. I think that Carlos Laza killed his wife for the insurance money, and to provide a scapegoat he invented a twin brother with a distinctive appearance, to be chased fruitlessly across the country while he remained here waiting for the policy payment to be granted."

"But the evidence left behind?"

Barham nodded. "All left by Carlos Laza. I believe he suffocated his wife and carried her jewels out to the well, the safest place he could think of to hide them temporarily. He then set about arranging the spare room where 'Rafael' had supposedly been staying to give evidence of a hasty departure and went out into the storm to leave behind the 'killer's' tracks, waiting until the snow had stopped falling before coming all the way into the village to report the murder."

Silver leaned forward. "But why the rigmarole about footprints at all? If he hadn't complicated matters with the second set of prints–prints that stopped halfway down the lane–then it all would have seemed much more straightforward, wouldn't it?"

"I think the snowfall took him by surprise. He realised the 'killer' would have left footprints in the snow when fleeing from the scene, so he had to go out and make them. He wouldn't dare walk all the way into the village and risk being seen, so he had to stop short, within shouting distance of the widow Lambe's cottage, trusting in the falling snow and her poor eyesight to make him invisible to her. He then turned about and immediately retraced his steps to the cottage. That would account for that first set of prints appearing smudged–the result of having to carefully but awkwardly place his feet inside the existing prints all the way back up the lane."

Constable Hake tutted. "And what's your proof for all this, then?"

"I have none. I would suggest, however, that Inspector Ainsworthy would do well to try to locate the supposed letter from Faversham telling of Rafael Laza's imminent arrival–did anyone in the village actually see the letter?–and to learn if anyone meeting his description was indeed seen in Faversham in the weeks leading up to the murder. Most of all, I would suggest searching the Lazas' well as soon as possible, to see what it might contain."

"I think," Hake said heavily, "the inspector ought to hear from you about this himself..."

Owen Barham submitted meekly to be led into the barparlour, where he went through his reasoning on the theft and murder once more under the stony gazes of the men from the County Constabulary. Silver meanwhile puffed on his pipe and regaled his companions with tales of his own career as a private enquiry agent. With the information provided, Inspector Ainsworthy and his subordinates headed to the windmill, where the bucket drawn up from the well proved to contain a leather bag holding Mrs. Laza's missing jewelry. Confronted with this evidence, Carlos Laza panicked, and breaking free from a sergeant's restraining hand, plunged out a window and into the snowdrifts in an attempt to escape. He was finally brought down in a tackle and dragged back to the Old Sparrow Hawk between two constables.

Barham and Silver had by then retired to the cramped bed in the cramped room at the back of the inn, entirely missing the commotion attending the arrest, and were fast asleep.